OUT-OF-DOORS
IN THE
HOLY LAND

The Gate of David, Jerusalem.

OUT-OF-DOORS
IN
THE HOLY LAND

IMPRESSIONS OF TRAVEL
IN BODY AND SPIRIT

BY

HENRY VAN DYKE

ILLUSTRATED

NEW YORK

CHARLES SCRIBNER'S SONS

MDCCCCVIII

PREFACE

For a long time, in the hopefulness and confidence of youth, I dreamed of going to Palestine. But that dream was denied, for want of money and leisure.

Then, for a long time, in the hardening strain of early manhood, I was afraid to go to Palestine, lest the journey should prove a disenchantment, and some of my religious beliefs be rudely shaken, perhaps destroyed. But that fear was removed by a little voyage to the gates of death, where it was made clear to me that no belief is worth keeping unless it can bear the touch of reality.

In that year of pain and sorrow, through a full surrender to the Divine Will, the hopefulness and confidence of youth came back to me. Since then it has been possible once more to wake in the morning with the feeling that the day might bring something new and wonderful and welcome, and to travel into the future with a whole and happy heart.

This is what I call growing younger; though the

years increase, yet the burden of them is lessened, and the fear that life will some day lead into an empty prison-house has been cast out by the incoming of the Perfect Love.

So it came to pass that when a friend offered me, at last, the opportunity of going to Palestine if I would give him my impressions of travel for his magazine, I was glad to go. Partly because there was a piece of work,—a drama whose scene lies in Damascus and among the mountains of Samaria,—that I wanted to finish there; partly because of the expectancy that on such a journey any of the days might indeed bring something new and wonderful and welcome; but most of all because I greatly desired to live for a little while in the country of Jesus, hoping to learn more of the meaning of His life in the land where it was spent, and lost, and forever saved.

Here, then, you have the history of this little book, reader: and if it pleases you to look further into its pages, you can see for yourself how far my dreams and hopes were realised.

It is the record of a long journey in the spirit and

a short voyage in the body. If you find here impressions that are lighter, mingled with those that are deeper, that is because life itself is really woven of such contrasted threads. Even on a pilgrimage small adventures happen. Of the elders of Israel on Sinai it is written, "They saw God and did eat and drink"; and the Apostle Paul was not too much engrossed with his mission to send for the cloak and books and parchments that he left behind at Troas.

If what you read here makes you wish to go to the Holy Land, I shall be glad; and if you go in the right way, you surely will not be disappointed.

But there are two things in the book which I would not have you miss.

The first is the new conviction,—new at least to me,—that Christianity is an out-of-doors religion. From the birth in the grotto at Bethlehem (where Joseph and Mary took refuge because there was no room for them in the inn) to the crowning death on the hill of Calvary outside the city wall, all of its important events took place out-of-doors. Except the discourse in the upper chamber at Jerusalem, all of its great words, from the sermon on the mount to the last commission to the disciples, were spoken in the open air. How shall we understand it unless we carry it under the free sky and interpret it in the companionship of nature?

The second thing that I would have you find here is the deepened sense that Jesus Himself is the great, the imperishable miracle. His words are spirit and life. His character is the revelation of the Perfect Love. This was the something new and wonderful and welcome that came to me in Palestine: a simpler, clearer, surer view of the human life of God.

HENRY VAN DYKE.

AVALON,
JUNE 10, 1908.

CONTENTS

ILLUSTRATIONS

I

TRAVELLERS' JOY

I

INVITATION

WHO would not go to Palestine?

To look upon that little stage where the drama of humanity has centred in such unforgetable scenes; to trace the rugged paths and ancient highways along which so many heroic and pathetic figures have travelled; above all, to see with the eyes as well as with the heart

> "Those holy fields
> Over whose acres walked those blessed feet
> Which, nineteen hundred years ago, were nail'd
> For our advantage on the bitter cross"—

for the sake of these things who would not travel far and endure many hardships?

It is easy to find Palestine. It lies in the southeast corner of the Mediterranean coast, where the "sea in the midst of the nations," makes a great elbow between Asia Minor and Egypt. A tiny land, about a hundred and fifty miles long and

3

sixty miles wide, stretching in a fourfold band from the foot of snowy Hermon and the Lebanons to the fulvous crags of Sinai: a green strip of fertile plain beside the sea, a blue strip of lofty and broken highlands, a gray-and-yellow strip of sunken river-valley, a purple strip of high mountains rolling away to the Arabian desert. There are a dozen lines of steamships to carry you thither; a score of well-equipped agencies to conduct you on what they call "a *de luxe* religious expedition to Palestine."

But how to find the Holy Land—ah, that is another question.

Fierce and mighty nations, hundreds of human tribes, have trampled through that coveted corner of the earth, contending for its possession: and the fury of their fighting has swept the fields as with fire. Temples and palaces have vanished like tents from the hillside. The ploughshare of havoc has been driven through the gardens of luxury. Cities have risen and crumbled upon the ruins of older cities. Crust after crust of pious legend has formed over the deep valleys; and tradition has set up its altars "upon every high hill and under every

4

green tree." The rival claims of sacred places are fiercely disputed by churchmen and scholars. It is a poor prophet that has but one birthplace and one tomb.

And now, to complete the confusion, the hurried, nervous, comfort-loving spirit of modern curiosity has broken into Palestine, with railways from Jaffa to Jerusalem, from Mount Carmel to the Sea of Galilee, from Beirût to Damascus,—with macadamized roads to Shechem and Nazareth and Tiberias, —with hotels at all the "principal points of interest,"—and with every facility for doing Palestine in ten days, without getting away from the market-reports, the gossip of the *table d'hôte*, and all that queer little complex of distracting habits which we call civilization.

But the Holy Land which I desire to see can be found only by escaping from these things. I want to get away from them; to return into the long past, which is also the hidden present, and to lose myself a little there, to the end that I may find myself again. I want to make acquaintance with the soul of that land where so much that is strange and memorable and for ever beautiful has come to pass: to walk quietly and humbly, without much disputation or talk, in fellowship with the spirit that haunts those hills and vales, under the influence of that deep and lucent sky. I want to feel that ineffable charm which breathes from its mountains, meadows and streams: that charm which made the children of Israel in the desert long for it as a land flowing with milk and honey; and the great Prince Joseph in Eygpt require an oath of his brethren that they would lay his bones in the quiet vale of Shechem where he had fed his father's sheep; and the daughters of Jacob beside the rivers of Babylon mingle tears with their music when they remembered Zion.

There was something in that land, surely, some personal and indefinable spirit of place, which was known and loved by prophet and psalmist, and most of all by Him who spread His table on the green grass, and taught His disciples while they walked the narrow paths waist-deep in rustling wheat, and spoke His messages of love from a little boat rocking on the lake, and found His asylum of prayer high on the mountainside, and kept His parting-hour with His friends in the moon-silvered quiet of the garden of olives. That spirit of place, that soul of the Holy Land, is what I fain would meet on my pilgrimage,—for the sake of Him who interprets it in love. And I know well where to find it,—out-of-doors.

I will not sleep under a roof in Palestine, but nightly pitch my wandering tent beside some fountain, in some grove or garden, on some vacant threshing-floor, beneath the Syrian stars. I will not join myself to any company of labelled tourists hurrying with much discussion on their appointed itinerary, but take into fellowship three tried and trusty comrades, that we may enjoy solitude together. I will not seek to make any archæological discovery, nor to prove any theological theory, but simply to ride through the highlands of Judea, and the valley of Jordan, and the mountains of Gilead, and the rich plains of Samaria, and the grassy hills of Galilee, looking upon the faces and the ways of the common folk, the labours of the husbandman in the field, the vigils of the shepherd on the hillside, the games of the children in the market-place, and reaping

"The harvest of a quiet eye
That broods and sleeps on his own heart."

Four things, I know, are unchanged amid all the changes that have passed over the troubled and bewildered land. The cities have sunken into dust: the trees of the forest have fallen: the nations have dissolved. But the mountains keep their immutable outline: the liquid stars shine with the same light, move on the same pathways: and between the mountains and the stars, two other changeless things, frail and imperishable,—the flowers that flood the earth in every springtide, and the human heart where hopes and longings and affections and desires blossom immortally. Chiefly of these things, and of Him who gave them a new meaning, I will speak to you, reader, if you care to go with me out-of-doors in the Holy Land.

II

MOVING PICTURES

OF the voyage, made with all the swiftness and directness of one who seeks the shortest distance between two points, little remains in memory except a few moving pictures, vivid and half-real, as in a kinematograph.

First comes a long, swift ship, the *Deutschland*, quivering and rolling over the dull March waves of the Atlantic. Then the morning sunlight streams on the jagged rocks of the Lizard, where two wrecked steamships are hanging, and on the green headlands and gray fortresses of Plymouth. Then a soft, rosy sunset over the mole, the dingy houses, the tiled roofs, the cliffs, the misty-budded trees of Cherbourg. Then Paris at two in the morning: the lower quarters still stirring with somnambulistic life, the lines of lights twinkling placidly on the empty boulevards. Then a whirl through the *Bois* in a motor-car, a breakfast at Versailles with a merry little party of friends, a lazy walk through miles of picture-galleries

9

without a guide-book or a care. Then the night express for Italy, a glimpse of the Alps at sunrise, snow all around us, the thick darkness of the Mount Cenis tunnel, the bright sunshine of Italian spring, terraced hillsides, clipped and pollarded trees, waking vineyards and gardens, Turin, Genoa, Rome, arches of ruined aqueducts, snow upon the Southern Apennines, the blooming fields of Capua, umbrella-pines and silvery poplars, and at last, from my balcony at the hotel, the glorious curving panorama of the bay of Naples, Vesuvius without a cloud, and Capri like an azure lion couchant on the broad shield of the sea. So ends the first series of films, ten days from home.

After an intermission of twenty-four hours, the second series begins on the white ship *Oceana*, an immense yacht, ploughing through the tranquil, sapphire Mediterranean, with ten passengers on board, and the band playing three times a day just as usual. Then comes the low line of the African coast, the lighthouse of Alexandria, the top of Pompey's Pillar showing over the white, modern city.

Half a dozen little rowboats meet us, well out at

sea, buffeted and tossed by the waves: they are fishing: see! one of the men has a strike, he pulls in his trolling-line, hand over hand, very slowly, it seems, as the steamship rushes by. I lean over the side, run to the stern of the ship to watch,—hurrah, he pulls in a silvery fish nearly three feet long. Good luck to you, my Egyptian brother of the angle!

Now a glimpse of the crowded, busy harbour of Alexandria, (recalling memories of fourteen years ago,) and a leisurely trans-shipment to the little Khedivial steamer, *Prince Abbas*, with her Scotch officers, Italian stewards, Maltese doctor, Turkish sailors, and freight-handlers who come from whatever places it has pleased Heaven they should be born in. The freight is variegated, and the third-class passengers are a motley crowd.

A glance at the forward main-deck shows Egyptians in white cotton, and Turks in the red fez, and Arabs in white and brown, and coal-black Soudanese, and nondescript Levantines, and Russians in fur coats and lamb's-wool caps, and Greeks in blue embroidered jackets, and women in baggy trousers and black veils, and babies, and cats, and parrots.

11

Here is a tall, venerable grandfather, with spectacles and a long gray beard, dressed in a black robe with a hood and a yellow scarf; grave, patriarchal, imperturbable: his little granddaughter, a pretty elf of a child, with flower-like face and shining eyes, dances hither and yon among the chaos of freight and luggage; but as the chill of evening descends she takes shelter between his knees, under the folds of his long robe, and, while he feeds her with bread and sweetmeats, keeps up a running comment of remarks and laughter at all around her, and the unspeakable solemnity of old Father Abraham's face is lit up, now and then, with the flicker of a resistless smile.

Here are two bronzed Arabs of the desert, in striped burnoose and white kaftan, stretched out for the night upon their rugs of many colours. Between them lies their latest purchase, a brand-new patent carpet-sweeper, made in Ohio, and going, who knows where among the hills of Bashan.

A child dies in the night, on the voyage; in the morning, at anchor in the mouth of the Suez Canal, we hear the carpenter hammering together a little pine coffin. All day Sunday the indescribable traffic of Port Saïd passes around us; ships of all nations coming and going; a big German Lloyd boat just home from India crowded with troops in khâki, band playing, flags flying; huge dredgers, sombre, oxlike-looking things, with lines of incredibly dirty men in fluttering rags running up the gang-planks with bags of coal on their backs; rowboats shuttling to and fro between the ships and the huddled, transient, modern town, which is made up of curiosity shops, hotels, business houses and dens of iniquity; a row of Egyptian sail boats, with high prows, low sides, long lateen yards, ranged along the entrance to the canal. At sunset we steam past the big statue of Ferdinand de Lesseps, standing far out on the breakwater and pointing back with a dramatic gesture to his world-transforming ditch. Then we go dancing over the yellow waves into the full moonlight toward Palestine.

In the early morning I clamber on deck into a thunderstorm: wild west wind, rolling billows, flying gusts of rain, low clouds hanging over the sand-hills of the coast: a harbourless shore, far as eye can see, a land that makes no concession to the ocean with bay or inlet, but cries, "Hitherto shalt thou come, but no farther; and here shall thy proud waves be stayed." There are the flat-roofed houses, and the orange groves, and the minaret, and the lighthouse of Jaffa, crowning its rounded hill of rock. We are tossing at anchor a mile from the shore. Will the boats come out to meet us in this storm, or must we go on to Haifâ, fifty miles beyond? Rumour says that the police have refused to permit the boats to put out. But look, here they come, half a dozen open whale-boats, each manned by a dozen lusty, bare-legged, brown rowers, buffeting their way between the scattered rocks, leaping high on the crested waves. The chiefs of the crews scramble on board the steamer, identify the passengers consigned to the different tourist-agencies, sort out the baggage and lower it into the boats.

My tickets, thus far, have been provided by the great Cook, and I fall to the charge of his head boatman, a dusky demon of energy. A slippery climb down the swaying ladder, a leap into the arms of two sturdy rowers, a stumble over the wet thwarts, and I

Jaffa.

The port where King Solomon landed his cedar beams from Lebanon for the building of the Temple.

find myself in the stern sheets of the boat. A young Dutchman follows with stolid suddenness. Two Italian gentlemen, weeping, refuse to descend more than half-way, climb back, and are carried on to Haifâ. A German lady with a parrot in a cage comes next, and her anxiety for the parrot makes her forget to be afraid. Then comes a little Polish lady, evidently a bride; she shuts her eyes tight and drops into the boat, pale, silent, resolved that she will not scream: her husband follows, equally pale, and she clings indifferently to his hand and to mine, her eyes still shut, a pretty image of white courage. The boat pushes off; the rowers smite the waves with their long oars and sing "Halli—yallah—yah hallah"; the steersman high in the stern shouts unintelligible (and, I fear, profane) directions; we are swept along on the tops of the waves, between the foaming rocks, drenched by spray and flying showers: at last we bump alongside the little quay, and climb out on the wet, gliddery stones.

The kinematograph pictures are ended, for I am in Palestine, on the first of April, just fifteen days from home.

III

RENDEZVOUS

WILL my friends be here to meet me, I wonder?
This is the question which presses upon me more
closely than anything else, I must confess, as I set
foot for the first time upon the sacred soil of Palestine. I know that this is not as it should be. All the
conventions of travel require the pilgrim to experience a strange curiosity and excitement, a profound
emotion, "a supreme anguish," as an Italian writer
describes it, "in approaching this land long dreamed
about, long waited for, and almost despaired of."

But the conventions of travel do not always correspond to the realities of the heart. Your first sight
of a place may not be your first perception of it: that
may come afterward, in some quiet, unexpected
moment. Emotions do not follow a time-table; and
I propose to tell no lies in this book. My strongest
feeling as I enter Jaffa is the desire to know whether
my chosen comrades have come to the rendezvous
at the appointed time, to begin our long ride together.

It is a remote and uncertain combination, I grant you. The Patriarch, a tall, slender youth of seventy years, whose home is beside the Golden Gate of California, was wandering among the ruins of Sicily when I last heard from him. The Pastor and his wife, the Lady of Walla Walla, who live on the shores of Puget Sound, were riding camels across the peninsula of Sinai and steamboating up the Nile. Have the letters, the cablegrams that were sent to them been safely delivered? Have the hundreds of unknown elements upon which our combination depended been working secretly together for its success? Has our proposal been according to the supreme disposal, and have all the roads been kept clear by which we were hastening from three continents to meet on the first day of April at the *Hotel du Parc* in Jaffa?

Yes, here are my three friends, in the quaint little garden of the hotel, with its purple-flowering vines of Bougainvillea, fragrant orange-trees, drooping palms, and long-tailed cockatoos drowsing on their perches. When people really know each other an unfamiliar meeting-place lends a singular intimacy

17

and joy to the meeting. There is a surprise in it, no matter how long and carefully it has been planned. There are a thousand things to talk of, but at first nothing will come except the wonder of getting together. The sight of the desired faces, unchanged beneath their new coats of tan, is a happy assurance that personality is not a dream. The touch of warm hands is a sudden proof that friendship is a reality.

Presently it begins to dawn upon us that there is something wonderful in the place of our conjunction, and we realise dimly,—very dimly, I am sure, and yet with a certain vague emotion of reverence,— where we are.

"We came yesterday," says the Lady, "and in the afternoon we went to see the House of Simon the Tanner, where they say the Apostle Peter lodged."

"Did it look like the real house?"

"Ah," she answers smilingly, "how do I know? They say there are two of them. But what do I care? It is certain that we are here. And I think that St. Peter was here once, too, whether the house he lived in is standing yet, or not."

Yes, that is reasonably certain; and this is the place where he had his strange vision of a religion meant for all sorts and conditions of men. It is certain, also, that this is the port where Solomon landed his beams of cedar from Lebanon for the building of the Temple, and that the Emperor Vespasian sacked the town, and that Richard Lionheart planted the banner of the crusade upon its citadel. But how far away and dreamlike it all seems, on this spring morning, when the wind is tossing the fronds of the palm-trees, and the gleams of sunshine are flying across the garden, and the last clouds of the broken thunderstorm are racing westward through the blue toward the highlands of Judea.

Here is our new friend, the dragoman George Cavalcanty, known as "Telhami," the Bethlehemite, standing beside us in the shelter of the orange-trees: a trim, alert figure, in his belted suit of khâki and his riding-boots of brown leather.

"Is everything ready for the journey, George?"

"Everything is prepared, according to the instructions you sent from Avalon. The tents are pitched a little beyond Latrûn, twenty miles away. The horses are waiting at Ramleh. After you have had your mid-day breakfast, we will drive there in carriages, and get into the saddle, and ride to our own camp before the night falls."

A PSALM OF THE DISTANT ROAD

Happy is the man that seeth the face of a friend in
    a far country:
The darkness of his heart is melted in the rising of
    an inward joy.

It is like the sound of music heard long ago and half
    forgotten:
It is like the coming back of birds to a wood that
    winter hath made bare.

I knew not the sweetness of the fountain till I found
    it flowing in the desert:
Nor the value of a friend till the meeting in a lonely
    land.

The multitude of mankind had bewildered me and
    oppressed me:
And I said to God, Why hast thou made the world
    so wide?

But when my friend came the wideness of the world
    had no more terror:
Because we were glad together among men who knew
    us not.

21

*I was slowly reading a book that was written in
a strange language:*
*And suddenly I came upon a page in mine own
familiar tongue.*

*This was the heart of my friend that quietly under-
stood me:*
*The open heart whose meaning was clear without a
word.*

*O my God whose love followeth all thy pilgrims
and strangers:*
*I praise thee for the comfort of comrades on a distant
road.*

II

GOING UP TO JERUSALEM

I

"THE EXCELLENCY OF SHARON"

YOU understand that what we had before us in this first stage of our journey was a very simple proposition. The distance from Jaffa to Jerusalem is fifty miles by railway and forty miles by carriage-road. Thousands of pilgrims and tourists travel it every year; and most of them now go by the train in about four hours, with advertised stoppages of three minutes at Lydda, eight minutes at Ramleh, ten minutes at Sejed, and unadvertised delays at the convenience of the engine. But we did not wish to get our earliest glimpse of Palestine from a car-window, nor to begin our travels in a mechanical way. The first taste of a journey often flavours it to the very end.

The old highroad, which is now much less frequented than formerly, is very fair as far as Ramleh; and beyond that it is still navigable for vehicles, though somewhat broken and billowy. Our plan, therefore, was to drive the first ten miles, where the road was flat and uninteresting, and then ride the rest of the way. This would enable us to avoid the advertised rapidity and the uncertain delays of the railway, and bring us quietly through the hills, about the close of the second day, to the gates of Jerusalem.

The two victorias rattled through the streets of Jaffa, past the low, flat-topped Oriental houses, the queer little open shops, the orange-groves in full bloom, the palm-trees waving their plumes over garden-walls, and rolled out upon the broad highroad across the fertile, gently undulating Plain of Sharon. On each side were the neat, well-cultivated fields and vegetable-gardens of the German colonists belonging to the sect of the Templers. They are a people of antique theology and modern agriculture. Believing that the real Christianity is to be found in the Old Testament rather than in the New, they propose to begin the social and religious reformation of the world by a return to the programme of the Minor Prophets. But meantime they conduct their farming operations in a very profitable way. Their grain-fields, their fruit-orchards, their vegetable-gardens are trim and orderly, and they make an excellent wine, which they call "The Treasure of Zion." Their effect upon the landscape, however, is conventional.

But in spite of the presence and prosperity of the Templers, the spirit of the scene through which we passed was essentially Oriental. The straggling hedges of enormous cactus, the rows of plumy euca-lyptus-trees, the budding figs and mulberries, gave it a semi-tropical touch and along the highway we encountered fragments of the leisurely, dishevelled, dignified East: grotesque camels, pensive donkeys carrying incredible loads, flocks of fat-tailed sheep and lop-eared goats, bronzed peasants in flowing garments, and white-robed women with veiled faces.

Beneath the tall tower of the forty martyrs at Ram-leh (Mohammedan or Christian, their names are for-gotten) we left the carriages, loaded our luggage on the three pack-mules, mounted our saddle-horses, and rode on across the plain, one of the fruitful gardens and historic battle-fields of the world. Here the hosts of the Israelites and the Philistines, the Egyptians and the Romans, the Persians and the Arabs, the Crusaders and the Saracens, have marched and contended. But as we passed through the sun-showers and rain-showers of an April afternoon, all was tranquillity and beauty on every side. The rolling fields were embroidered with innumerable flowers. The narcissus, the "rose of Sharon," had faded. But the little blue "lilies-of-the-valley" were there, and the pink and saffron mallows, and the yellow and white daisies, and the violet and snow of the drooping cyclamen, and the gold of the genesta, and the orange-red of the pimpernel, and, most beautiful of all, the glowing scarlet of the numberless anemones. Wide acres of young wheat and barley glistened in the light, as the wind-waves rippled through their short, silken blades. There were few trees, except now and then an olive-orchard or a round-topped carob with its withered pods.

The highlands of Judea lay stretched out along the eastern horizon, a line of azure and amethystine heights, changing colour and seeming almost to breathe and move as the cloud shadows fleeted over them, and reaching away northward and southward as far as eye could see. Rugged and treeless, save for a clump of oaks or terebinths planted here or

The Tall Tower of the Forty Martyrs at Ramleh.

there around some Mohammedan saint's tomb, they would have seemed forbidding but that their slopes were clothed with the tender herbage of spring, their outlines varied with deep valleys and blue gorges, and all their mighty bulwarks jewelled right royally with the opalescence of sunset.

In a hollow of the green plain to the left we could see the white houses and the yellow church tower of Lydda, the supposed burial-place of Saint George of Cappadocia, who killed the dragon and became the patron saint of England. On a conical hill to the right shone the tents of the Scotch explorer who is excavating the ancient city of Gezer, which was the dowry of Pharaoh's daughter when she married King Solomon. City, did I say? At least four cities are packed one upon another in that grassy mound, the oldest going back to the flint age; and yet if you should examine their site and measure their ruins, you would feel sure that none of them could ever have amounted to anything more than what we should call a poor little town.

It came upon us gently but irresistibly that after-noon, as we rode easily across the land of the Philistines in a few hours, that we had never really read the Old Testament as it ought to be read,—as a book written in an Oriental atmosphere, filled with the glamour, the imagery, the magniloquence of the East. Unconsciously we had been reading it as if it were a collection of documents produced in Heidelberg, Germany, or in Boston, Massachusetts: precise, literal, scientific.

We had been imagining the Philistines as a mighty nation, and their land as a vast territory filled with splendid cities and ruled by powerful monarchs. We had been trying to understand and interpret the stories of their conflict with Israel as if they had been written by a Western war-correspondent, careful to verify all his statistics and meticulous in the exact description of all his events. This view of things melted from us with a gradual surprise as we realised that the more deeply we entered into the poetry, the closer we should come to the truth, of the narrative. Its moral and religious meaning is firm and steadfast as the mountains round about Jerusalem; but even as those mountains rose before us glorified, uplifted, and bejewelled by the vague splendours of the sunset, so the form of the history was enlarged and its colours irradiated by the figurative spirit of the East.

There at our feet, bathed in the beauty of the evening air, lay the Valley of Aijalon, where Joshua fought with the "five kings of the Amorites," and broke them and chased them. The "kings" were headmen of scattered villages, chiefs of fierce and ragged tribes. But the fighting was hard, and as Joshua led his wild clansmen down upon them from the ascent of Beth-horon, he feared the day might be too short to win the victory. So he cheered the hearts of his men with an old war-song from the Book of Jasher.

"Sun, stand thou still upon Gibeon;
And thou, moon, in the Valley of Aijalon.
And the sun stood still, and the moon stayed,
Until the nation had avenged themselves of their enemies."

Does any one suppose that this is intended to teach us that the sun moves and that on this day his course was arrested? Must we believe that the whole solar system was dislocated for the sake of this battle? To understand the story thus is to misunderstand its vital spirit. It is poetry, imagination, heroism. By the new courage that came into the hearts of Israel with their leader's song, the Lord shortened the conflict to fit the day, and the sunset and the moonrise saw the Valley of Aijalon swept clean of Israel's foes.

As we passed through the wretched, mud-built village of Latrûn (said to be the birthplace of the Penitent Thief), a dozen long-robed Arabs were earnestly discussing some question of municipal interest in the grassy market-place. They were as grave as the storks, in their solemn plumage of black and white, which were parading philosophically along the edge of a marsh to our right. A couple of jackals slunk furtively across the road ahead of us in the dusk. A *kafila* of long-necked camels undulated over the plain. The shadows fell more heavily over cactus-hedge and olive-orchard as we turned down the hill.

In the valley night had come. The large, trembling stars were strewn through the vault above us, and rested on the dim ridges of the mountains, and shone reflected in the puddles of the long road like fallen jewels. The lights of Latrûn, if it had any, were already out of sight behind us. Our horses were weary and began to stumble. Where was the camp?

Look, there is a light, bobbing along the road toward us. It is Youssouf, our faithful major-domo, come out with a lantern to meet us. A few rods farther through the mud, and we turn a corner beside an acacia hedge and the ruined arch of an ancient well. There, in a little field of flowers, close to the tiniest of brooks, our tents are waiting for us with open doors. The candles are burning on the table. The rugs are spread and the beds are made. The dinner-table is laid for four, and there is a bright bunch of flowers in the middle of it. We have seen the excellency of Sharon and the moon is shining for us on the Valley of Aijalon.

II

"THE STRENGTH OF THE HILLS"

It is no hardship to rise early in camp. At the windows of a house the daylight often knocks as an unwelcome messenger, rousing the sleeper with a sudden call. But through the roof and the sides of a tent it enters gently and irresistibly, embracing you with soft arms, laying rosy touches on your eyelids; and while your dream fades you know that you are awake and it is already day.

As we lift the canvas curtains and come out of our pavilions, the sun is just topping the eastern hills, and all the field around us glittering with immense drops of dew. On the top of the ruined arch beside the camp our Arab watchman, hired from the village of Latrûn as we passed, is still perched motionless, wrapped in his flowing rags, holding his long gun across his knees.

"*Salâm 'aleikum, yâ ghafîr!*" I say, and though my Arabic is doubtless astonishingly bad, he knows my meaning; for he answers gravely, "'*Aleikum essalâm!*—And with you be peace!"

It is indeed a peaceful day in which our journey to Jerusalem is completed. Leaving the tents and impedimenta in charge of Youssouf and Shukari the cook, and the muleteers, we are in the saddle by seven o'clock, and riding into the narrow entrance of the Wâdi 'Ali. It is a long, steep valley leading into the heart of the hills. The sides are ribbed with rocks, among which the cyclamens grow in profusion. A few olives are scattered along the bottom of the vale, and at the tomb of the Imâm 'Ali there is a grove of large trees. At the summit of the pass we rest for half an hour, to give our horses a breathing-space, and to refresh our eyes with the glorious view westward over the tumbled country of the Shephelah, the opalescent Plain of Sharon, the sand-hills of the coast, and the broad blue of the Mediterranean. Northward and southward and eastward the rocky summits and ridges of Judea roll away.

Now we understand what the Psalmist means by ascribing "the strength of the hills" to Jehovah; and a new light comes into the song:

> "As the mountains are round about Jerusalem,
> So Jehovah is round about his people."

These natural walls and terraces of gray limestone have the air of antique fortifications and watch-towers of the border. They are truly "munitions of rocks." Chariots and horsemen could find no field for their manœuvres in this broken and perpendicular country. Entangled in these deep and winding valleys by which they must climb up from the plain, the invaders would be at the mercy of the light infantry of the highlands, who would roll great stones upon them as they passed through the narrow defiles, and break their ranks by fierce and sudden downward rushes as they toiled panting up the steep hillsides. It was this strength of the hills that the children of Israel used for the defence of Jerusalem, and by this they were able to resist and defy the Philistines, whom they could never wholly conquer.

Yonder on the hillside, as we ride onward, we see a reminder of that old tribal warfare between the people of the highlands and the people of the plains. That gray village, perched upon a rocky ridge above thick olive-orchards and a deliciously green valley, is the ancient Kirjath-Jearim, where the Ark of Jehovah was hidden for twenty years, after the Philistines had sent back this perilous trophy of their victory over the sons of Eli, being terrified by the pestilence and disaster that followed its possession. The men of Beth-shemesh, to whom it was first returned, were afraid to keep it, because they also had been smitten with death when they dared to peep into this dreadful box. But the men of Kirjath-

Jearim were at once bolder and wiser, so they "came and fetched up the Ark of Jehovah, and brought it into the house of Abinadab in the hill, and set apart Eleazar, his son, to keep the Ark of Jehovah."

What strange vigils in that little hilltop cottage where the young man watches over this precious, dangerous, gilded coffer, while Saul is winning and losing his kingdom in a turmoil of blood and sorrow and madness, forgetful of Israel's covenant with the Most High! At last comes King David, from his newly won stronghold of Zion, seeking eagerly for this lost symbol of the people's faith. "Lo, we heard of it at Ephratah; we found it in the field of the wood." So the gray stone cottage on the hilltop gave up its sacred treasure, and David carried it away with festal music and dancing. But was Eleazar glad, I wonder, or sorry, that his long vigil was ended?

To part from a care is sometimes like losing a friend.

I confess that it is difficult to make these ancient stories of peril and adventure, (or even the modern history of Abu Ghôsh the robber-chief of this village

a hundred years ago), seem real to us to-day. Everything around us is so safe and tranquil, and, in spite
of its novelty, so familiar. The road descends steeply
with long curves and windings into the Wâdi Beit
Hanîna. We meet and greet many travellers, on
horseback, in carriages and afoot, natives and pilgrims, German colonists, French priests, Italian
monks, English tourists and explorers. It is a pleasant game to guess from an approaching pilgrim's
looks whether you should salute him with "*Guten
Morgen*," or "*Buon' Giorno*," or "*Bon jour, m'sieur*."
The country people answer your salutation with a
pretty phrase: "*Nehârak   saîd   umubârak*—May
your day be happy and blessed."

At Kalôniyeh, in the bottom of the valley, there is
a prosperous settlement of German Jews; and the
gardens and orchards are flourishing. There is also
a little wayside inn, a rude stone building, with a terrace around it; and there, with apricots and plums
blossoming beside us, we eat our lunch *al fresco*, and
watch our long pack-train, with the camp and baggage, come winding down the hill and go tinkling
past us toward Jerusalem.

The place is very friendly; we are in no haste to leave it. A few miles to the southward, sheltered in the lap of a rounding hill, we can see the tall cypress-trees and quiet gardens of 'Ain Karîm, the village where John the Baptist was born. It has a singular air of attraction, seen from a distance, and one of the sweetest stories in the world is associated with it. For it was there that the young bride Mary visited her older cousin Elizabeth,—you remember the exquisite picture of the "Visitation" by Albertinelli in the Uffizi at Florence,—and the joy of coming motherhood in these two women's hearts spoke from each to each like a bell and its echo. Would the birth of Jesus, the character of Jesus, have been possible unless there had been the virginal and expectant soul of such a woman as Mary, ready to welcome His coming with her song? "My soul doth magnify the Lord, and my spirit hath rejoiced in God my Saviour." Does not the advent of a higher manhood always wait for the hope and longing of a nobler womanhood?

The chiming of the bells of St. John floats faintly and silverly across the valley as we leave the shelter of the wayside rest-house and mount for the last stage of our upward journey. The road ascends steeply. Nestled in the ravine to our left is the grizzled and dilapidated village of Liftâ, a town with an evil reputation.

"These people sold all their land," says George the dragoman, "twenty years ago, sold all the fields, gardens, olive-groves. Now they are dirty and lazy in that village,—all thieves!"

Over the crest of the hill the red-tiled roofs of the first houses of Jerusalem are beginning to appear. They are houses of mercy, it seems: one an asylum for the insane, the other a home for the aged poor. Passing them, we come upon schools and hospital buildings and other evidences of the charity of the Rothschilds toward their own people. All around us are villas and consulates, and rows of freshly built houses for Jewish colonists.

This is not at all the way that we had imagined to ourselves the first sight of the Holy City. All here is half-European, unromantic, not very picturesque. It may not be "the New Jerusalem," but it is certainly a modern Jerusalem. Here, in these com-

fortably commonplace dwellings, is almost half the
present population of the city; and rows of new
houses are rising on every side.

But look down the southward-sloping road. There
is the sight that you have imagined and longed to see:
the brown battlements, the white-washed houses, the
flat roofs, the slender minarets, the many-coloured
domes of the ancient city of David, and Solomon,
and Hezekiah, and Herod, and Omar, and Godfrey,
and Saladin,—but never of Christ. That great black
dome is the Church of the Holy Sepulchre. The one
beyond it is the Mosque of Omar. Those golden
bulbs and pinnacles beyond the city are the Greek
Church of Saint Mary Magdalen on the side of the
Mount of Olives; and on the top of the lofty ridge
rises the great pointed tower of the Russians from
which a huge bell booms out a deep-toned note of
welcome.

On every side we see the hospices and convents
and churches and palaces of the different sects of
Christendom. The streets are full of people and
carriages and beasts of burden. The dust rises
around us. We are tired with the trab, trab, trab of

our horses' feet upon the hard highroad. Let us not go into the confusion of the city, but ride quietly down to the left into a great olive-grove, outside the Damascus Gate.

Here our white tents are pitched among the trees, with the dear flag of our home flying over them. Here we shall find leisure and peace to unite our hearts, and bring our thoughts into tranquil harmony, before we go into the bewildering city. Here the big stars will look kindly down upon us through the silvery leaves, and the sounds of human turmoil and contention will not trouble us. The distant booming of the bell on the Mount of Olives will mark the night-hours for us, and the long-drawn plaintive call of the muezzin from the minaret of the little mosque at the edge of the grove will wake us to the sunrise.

A PSALM OF THE WELCOME TENT

This is the thanksgiving of the weary:
The song of him that is ready to rest.

It is good to be glad when the day is declining:
And the setting of the sun is like a word of peace.

The stars look kindly on the close of a journey:
The tent says welcome when the day's march is done.

For now is the time of the laying down of burdens:
And the cool hour cometh to them that have borne
the heat.

I have rejoiced greatly in labour and adventure:
My heart hath been enlarged in the spending of my
strength.

Now it is all gone yet I am not impoverished:
For thus only may I inherit the treasure of repose.

Blessed be the Lord that teacheth my hands to un-
close and my fingers to loosen:
He also giveth comfort to the feet that are washed
from the dust of the way.

*Blessed be the Lord that maketh my meat at nightfall
    savoury:*
*And filleth my evening cup with the wine of good
    cheer.*

*Blessed be the Lord that maketh me happy to be
    quiet:*
*Even as a child that cometh softly to his mother's
    lap.*

*O God thou faintest not neither is thy strength worn
    away with labour:*
*But it is good for us to be weary that we may obtain
    thy gift of rest.*

III

THE GATES OF ZION

I

A CITY THAT IS SET ON A HILL

OUT of the medley of our first impressions of Jerusalem one fact emerges like an island from the sea: it is a city that is lifted up. No river; no harbour; no encircling groves and gardens; a site so lonely and so lofty that it breathes the very spirit of isolation and proud self-reliance.

> "Beautiful in elevation, the joy of the whole earth
>   Is Mount Zion, on the sides of the north
>   The city of the great King."

Thus sang the Hebrew poet; and his song, like all true poetry, has the accuracy of the clearest vision. For this is precisely the one beauty that crowns Jerusalem: the beauty of a high place and all that belongs to it: clear sky, refreshing air, a fine outlook, and that indefinable sense of exultation that comes into the heart of man when he climbs a little nearer to the stars.

Twenty-five hundred feet above the level of the

sea is not a great height; but I can think of no other
ancient and world-famous city that stands as high.
Along the mountainous plateau of Judea, between
the sea-coast plain of Philistia and the sunken valley
of the Jordan, there is a line of sacred sites,—Beër-
sheba, Hebron, Bethlehem, Bethel, Shiloh, Shechem.
Each of them marks the place where a town grew up
around an altar. The central link in this chain of
shrine-cities is Jerusalem. Her form and outline,
her relation to the landscape and to the land, are
unchanged from the days of her greatest glory. The
splendours of her Temple and her palaces, the glitter
of her armies, the rich colour and glow of her abound-
ing wealth, have vanished. But though her garments are frayed and weather-worn, though she is an
impoverished and dusty queen, she still keeps her
proud position and bearing; and as you approach
her by the ancient road along the ridges of Judea
you see substantially what Sennacherib, and Nebu-
chadnezzar, and the Roman Titus must have seen.

"The sides of the north" slope gently down to the
huge gray wall of the city, with its many towers and
gates. Within those bulwarks, which are thirty-

eight feet high and two and a half miles in circumference, "Jerusalem is builded as a city that is compact together," covering with her huddled houses and crooked, narrow streets, the two or three rounded hills and shallow depressions in which the northern plateau terminates. South and east and west, the valley of the Brook Kidron and the Valley of Himmon surround the city wall with a dry moat three or four hundred feet deep.

Imagine the knuckles of a clenched fist, extended toward the south: that is the site of Jerusalem, impregnable, (at least in ancient warfare), from all sides except the north, where the wrist joins it to the higher tableland. This northern approach, open to Assyria, and Babylon, and Damascus, and Persia, and Greece, and Rome, has always been the weak point of Jerusalem. She was no unassailable fortress of natural strength, but a city lifted up, a lofty shrine, whose refuge and salvation were in Jehovah,—in the faith, the loyalty, the courage which flowed into the heart of her people from their religion. When these failed, she fell.

Jerusalem is no longer, and never again will be,

the capital of an earthly kingdom. But she is still one of the high places of the world, exalted in the imagination and the memory of Jews and Christians and Mohammedans, a metropolis of infinite human hopes and longings and devotions. Hither come the innumerable companies of foot-weary pilgrims, climbing the steep roads from the sea-coast, from the Jordan, from Bethlehem,—pilgrims who seek the place of the Crucifixion, pilgrims who would weep beside the walls of their vanished Temple, pilgrims who desire to pray where Mohammed prayed. Century after century these human throngs have assembled from far countries and toiled upward to this open, lofty plateau, where the ancient city rests upon the top of the closed hand, and where the ever-changing winds from the desert and the sea sweep and shift over the rocky hilltops, the mute, gray battlements, and the domes crowned with the cross, the crescent, and the star.

"The wind bloweth where it will, and thou hearest the voice thereof, but knowest not whence it cometh, nor whither it goeth; so is every one that is born of the Spirit."

THE GATES OF ZION

The mystery of the heart of mankind, the spiritual airs that breathe through it, the desires and aspirations that impel men in their journeyings, the common hopes that bind them together in companies, the fears and hatreds that array them in warring hosts,—there is no place in the world to-day where you can feel all this so deeply, so inevitably, so overwhelmingly, as at the Gates of Zion.

It is a feeling of confusion, at first: a bewildering sense of something vast and old and secret, speaking many tongues, taking many forms, yet never fully revealing its source and its meaning. The Jews, Mohammedans, and Christians who flock to those gates are alike in their sincerity, in their devotion, in the spirit of sacrifice that leads them on their pilgrimage. Among them all there are hypocrites and bigots, doubtless, but there are also earnest and devout souls, seeking something that is higher than themselves, "a city set upon a hill." Why do they not understand one another? Why do they fight and curse one another? Do they not all come to humble themselves, to pray, to seek the light?

Dark walls that embrace so many tear-stained,

51

blood-stained, holy and dishonoured shrines! And you, narrow and gloomy gates, through whose portals so many myriads of mankind have passed with their swords, their staves, their burdens and their palm-branches! What songs of triumph you have heard, what yells of battle-rage, what moanings of despair, what murmurs of hopes and gratitude, what cries of anguish, what bursts of careless, happy laughter,— all borne upon the wind that bloweth where it will across these bare and rugged heights. We will not seek to enter yet into the mysteries that you hide. We will tarry here for a while in the open sunlight, where the cool breeze of April stirs the olive-groves outside the Damascus Gate. We will tranquillize our thoughts,—perhaps we may even find them growing clearer and surer,—among the simple cares and pleasures that belong to the life of every day; the life which must have food when it is hungry, and rest when it is weary, and a shelter from the storm and the night; the life of those who are all strangers and sojourners upon the earth, and whose richest houses and strongest cities are, after all, but a little longer-lasting tents and camps.

II

THE CAMP IN THE OLIVE-GROVE

THE place of our encampment is peaceful and friendly, without being remote or secluded. The grove is large and free from all undergrowth: the trunks of the ancient olive-trees are gnarled and massive, the foliage soft and tremulous. The corner that George has chosen for us is raised above the road by a kind of terrace, so that it is not too easily accessible to the curious passer-by. Across the road we see a gray stone wall, and above it the roof of the Anglican Bishop's house, and the schools, from which a sound of shrill young voices shouting in play or chanting in unison rises at intervals through the day. The ground on which we stand is slightly furrowed with the little ridges of last year's ploughing: but it has not yet been broken this spring, and it is covered with millions of infinitesimal flowers, blue and purple and yellow and white, like tiny pansies run wild.

The four tents, each circular and about fifteen feet

53

in diameter, are arranged in a crescent. The one
nearest to the road is for the kitchen and service;
there Shukari, our Maronite *chef*, in his white cap
and apron, turns out an admirable six-course dinner
on a portable charcoal range not three feet square.
Around the door of this tent there is much coming
and going: edibles of all kinds are brought for sale;
visitors squat in sociable conversation; curious children hang about, watching the proceedings, or waiting for the favours which a good cook can bestow.

The next tent is the dining-room; the huge wooden
chests of the canteen, full of glass and china and
table-linen and new Britannia-ware, which shines
like silver, are placed one on each side of the entrance; behind the central tent-pole stands the din-
ing-table, with two chairs at the back and one at each
end, so that we can all enjoy the view through the
open door. The tent is lofty and lined with many-
coloured cotton cloth, arranged in elaborate patterns,
scarlet and green and yellow and blue. When the
four candles are lighted on the well-spread table, and
Youssouf the Greek, in his embroidered jacket and
baggy blue breeches, comes in to serve the dinner, it

is quite an Oriental scene. His assistant, Little Youssouf, the Copt, squats outside of the tent, at one side of the door, to wash up the dishes and polish the Britannia-ware.

The two other tents are of the same pattern and the same gaudy colours within: each of them contains two little iron bedsteads, two Turkish rugs, two washstands, one dressing-table, and such baggage as we had imagined necessary for our comfort, piled around the tent-pole,—this by way of precaution, lest some misguided hand should be tempted to slip under the canvas at night and abstract an unconsidered trifle lying near the edge of the tent.

Of our own men I must say that we never had a suspicion, either of their honesty or of their good-humour. Not only the four who had most immediately to do with us, but also the two chief muleteers, Mohammed 'Ali and Moûsa, and the songful boy, Mohammed el Nâsan, who warbled an interminable Arabian ditty all day long, and Fâris and the two other assistants, were models of fidelity and willing service. They did not quarrel (except once, over the division of the mule-loads, in the mountains of Gil-

55

ead); they got us into no difficulties and subjected us to no blackmail from humbugging Bedouin chiefs. They are of a picturesque motley in costume and of a bewildering variety in creed—Anglican, Catholic, Coptic, Maronite, Greek, Mohammedan, and one of whom the others say that "he belongs to no religion, but sings beautiful Persian songs." Yet, so far as we are concerned, they all do the things they ought to do and leave undone the things they ought not to do, and their way with us is peace. Much of this, no doubt, is due to the wisdom, tact, and firmness of George the Bethlehemite, the best of dragomans.

We have many visitors at the camp, but none unwelcome. The American Consul, a genial scholar who knows Palestine by heart and has made valuable contributions to the archæology of Jerusalem, comes with his wife to dine with us in the open air. George's gentle wife and his two bright little boys, Howard and Robert, are with us often. Missionaries come to tell us of their labours and trials. An Arab hunter, with his long flintlock musket, brings us beautiful gray partridges which he has shot among the near-by hills. The stable-master comes day after day with strings of horses galloping through the grove; for our first mounts were not to our liking, and we are determined not to start on our longer ride until we have found steeds that suit us. Peasants from the country round about bring all sorts of things to sell—vegetables, and lambs, and pigeons, and old coins, and embroidered caps.

There are two men ploughing in a vineyard behind the camp, beyond the edge of the grove. The plough is a crooked stick of wood which scratches the surface of the earth. The vines are lying flat on the ground, still leafless, closely pruned: they look like big black snakes.

Women of the city, dressed in black and blue silks, with black mantles over their heads, come out in the afternoon to picnic among the trees. They sit in little circles on the grass, smoking cigarettes and eating sweetmeats. If they see us looking at them they draw the corners of their mantles across the lower part of their faces; but when they think themselves unobserved they drop their veils and regard us curiously with lustrous brown eyes.

One morning a procession of rustic women and

girls, singing with shrill voices, pass the camp on their way to the city to buy the bride's clothes for a wedding. At nightfall they return singing yet more loudly, and accompanied by men and boys firing guns into the air and shouting.

Another day a crowd of villagers go by. Their old Sheikh rides in the midst of them, with his white-and-gold turban, his long gray beard, his flowing robes of rich silk. He is mounted on a splendid white Arab horse, with arched neck and flaunting tail; and a beautiful, gaily dressed little boy rides behind him with both arms clasped around the old man's waist. They are going up to the city for the Mohammedan rite of circumcision.

Later in the day a Jewish funeral comes hurrying through the grove: some twenty or thirty men in flat caps trimmed with fur and gabardines of cotton velvet, purple, or yellow, or pink, chanting psalms as they march, with the body of the dead man wrapped in linen cloth and carried on a rude bier on their shoulders. They seem in haste, (because the hour is late and the burial must be made before sunset), perhaps a little indifferent, or almost joyful.

Certainly there is no sign of grief in their looks or their voices; for among them it is counted a fortunate thing to die in the Holy City and to be buried on the southern slope of the Valley of Jehoshaphat, where Gabriel is to blow his trumpet for the resurrection.

III

IN THE STREETS OF JERUSALEM

OUTSIDE the gates we ride, for the roads which encircle the city wall and lead off to the north and south and east and west, are fairly broad and smooth. But within the gates we walk, for the streets are narrow, steep and slippery, and to attempt them on horseback is to travel with an anxious mind.

Through the Jaffa Gate, indeed, you may easily ride, or even drive in your carriage: not through the gateway itself, which is a close and crooked alley, but through the great gap in the wall beside it, made for the German Emperor to pass through at the time of his famous imperial scouting-expedition in Syria in 1898. Thus following the track of the great Wil-

liam you come to the entrance of the Grand New
Hotel, among curiosity-shops and tourist-agencies,
where a multitude of bootblacks assure you that you
need "a shine," and *valets de place* press their ser-
vices upon you, and ingratiating young merchants
try to allure you into their establishments to purchase photographs or embroidered scarves or olive-
wood souvenirs of the Holy Land.

Come over to Cook's office, where we get our letters, and stand for a while on the little terrace with
the iron railing, looking at the motley crowd which
fills the place in front of the citadel. Groups of blue-
robed peasant women sit on the curbstone, selling
firewood and grass and vegetables. Their faces are
bare and brown, wrinkled with the sun and the wind.
Turkish soldiers in dark-green uniform, Greek priests
in black robes and stove-pipe hats, Bedouins in flowing cloaks of brown and white, pale-faced Jews with
velvet gabardines and curly ear-locks, Moslem
women in many-coloured silken garments and half-
transparent veils, British tourists with cork helmets
and white umbrellas, camels, donkeys, goats, and
sheep, jostle together in picturesque confusion.

A Street in Jerusalem.

There is a water-carrier with his shiny, dripping, bulbous goat-skin on his shoulders. There is an Arab of the wilderness with a young gazelle in his arms.

Now let us go down the greasy, gliddery steps of David Street, between the diminutive dusky shops with open fronts where all kinds of queer things to eat and to wear are sold, and all sorts of craftsmen are at work making shoes, and tin pans, and copper pots, and wooden seats, and little tables, and clothes of strange pattern. A turn to the left brings us into Christian Street and the New Bazaar of the Greeks, with its modern stores.

A turn to the right and a long descent under dark archways and through dirty, shadowy alleys brings us to the Place of Lamentations, beside the ancient foundation wall of the Temple, where the Jews come in the afternoon of Fridays and festival-days to lean their heads against the huge stones and murmur forth their wailings over the downfall of Jerusalem. "For the majesty that is departed," cries the leader, and the others answer: "We sit in solitude and mourn." "We pray Thee have mercy on Zion," cries the leader, and the others answer: "Gather the children of Jerusalem." With most of them it seems a perfunctory mourning; but there are two or three old men with the tears running down their faces as they kiss the smooth-worn stones.

We enter convents and churches, mosques and tombs. We trace the course of the traditional *Via Dolorosa*, and try to reconstruct in our imagination the probable path of that grievous journey from the judgment-hall of injustice to the Calvary of cruelty— a path which now lies buried far below the present level of the city.

One impression deepens in my mind with every hour: this was never Christ's city. The confusion, the shallow curiosity, the self-interest, the clashing prejudices, the inaccessibility of the idle and busy multitudes were the same in His day that they are now. It was not here that Jesus found the men and women who believed in Him and loved Him, but in the quiet villages, among the green fields, by the peaceful lake-shores. And it is not here that we shall find the clearest traces, the most intimate visions of Him, but away in the big out-of-doors, where the sky opens free above us, and the landscapes roll away to far horizons.

As we loiter about the city, now alone, now under the discreet and unhampering escort of the Bethlehemite; watching the Mussulmans at their dinner in some dingy little restaurant, where kitchen, store-room and banquet-hall are all in the same apartment, level and open to the street; pausing to bargain with an impassive Arab for a leather belt or with an ingratiating Greek for a string of amber beads; looking in through the unshuttered windows of the Jewish houses where the families are gathered in festal array for the household rites of Passover week; turning over the chaplets, and rosaries, and anklets, and bracelets of coloured glass and mother-of-pearl, and variegated stones, and curious beans and seed-pods in the baskets of the street-vendors around the Church of the Holy Sepulchre; stepping back into an archway to avoid a bag-footed camel, or a gaily caparisoned horse, or a heavy-laden donkey passing through a narrow street; exchanging a smile and an unintelligible friendly jest with a sweet-faced, careless child; listening to long

disputes between buyers and sellers in that resound-
ing Arab tongue which seems full of tragic indigna-
tion and wrath, while the eyes of the handsome
brown Bedouins who use it remain unsearchable
in their Oriental languor and pride; Jerusalem becomes to us more and more a symbol and epitome
of that which is changeless and transient, capricious
and inevitable, necessary and insignificant, interest-
ing and unsatisfying, in the unfinished tragi-comedy
of human life. There are times when it fascinates us
with its whirling charm. There are other times when
we are glad to ride away from it, to seek communion
with the great spirit of some antique prophet, or to
find the consoling presence of Him who spake the
words of the eternal life.

A PSALM OF GREAT CITIES

How wonderful are the cities that man hath builded:
Their walls are compacted of heavy stones,
And their lofty towers rise above the tree-tops.

Rome, Jerusalem, Cairo, Damascus,—
Venice, Constantinople, Moscow, Pekin,—
London, New York, Berlin, Paris, Vienna,—

These are the names of mighty enchantments:
They have called to the ends of the earth,
They have secretly summoned an host of servants.

They shine from far sitting beside great waters:
They are proudly enthroned upon high hills,
They spread out their splendour along the rivers.

Yet are they all the work of small patient fingers:
Their strength is in the hand of man,
He hath woven his flesh and blood into their glory.

The cities are scattered over the world like ant-hills:
Every one of them is full of trouble and toil,
And their makers run to and fro within them.

Abundance of riches is laid up in their store-houses:
Yet they are tormented with the fear of want,
The cry of the poor in their streets is exceeding bitter.

Their inhabitants are driven by blind perturbations:
They whirl sadly in the fever of haste,
Seeking they know not what, they pursue it fiercely.

The air is heavy-laden with their breathing:
The sound of their coming and going is never still,
Even in the night I hear them whispering and crying.

Beside every ant-hill I behold a monster crouching:
This is the ant-lion Death,
He thrusteth forth his tongue and the people perish.

O God of wisdom thou hast made the country:
Why hast thou suffered man to make the town?

Then God answered, Surely I am the maker of man:
And in the heart of man I have set the city.

IV

MIZPAH AND THE MOUNT OF OLIVES

I

THE JUDGMENT-SEAT OF SAMUEL

MIZPAH of Benjamin stands to the northwest: the sharpest peak in the Judean range, crowned with a ragged, dusty village and a small mosque. We rode to it one morning over the steepest, stoniest bridle-paths that we had ever seen. The country was bleak and rocky, a skeleton of landscape; but between the stones and down the precipitous hillsides and along the hot gorges, the incredible multitude of spring flowers were abloom.

It was a stiff scramble up the conical hill to the little hamlet at the top, built out of and among ruins. The mosque, evidently an old Christian church remodelled, was bare, but fairly clean, cool, and tranquil. We peered through a grated window, tied with many-coloured scraps of rags by the Mohammedan pilgrims, into a whitewashed room containing a huge sarcophagus said to be the tomb of Samuel. Then we climbed the minaret and lingered on the tiny railed balcony, feeding on the view.

The peak on which we stood was isolated by deep ravines from the other hills of desolate gray and scanty green. Beyond the western range lay the Valley of Aijalon, and beyond that the rich Plain of Sharon with iridescent hues of green and blue and silver, and beyond that the yellow line of the sand-dunes broken by the white spot of Jaffa, and beyond that the azure breadth of the Mediterranean. Northward, at our feet, on the summit of a lower conical hill, ringed with gray rock, lay the village of El-Jib, the ancient Geba of Benjamin, one of the cities which Joshua gave to the Levites.

This was the place from which Jonathan and his armour-bearer set out, without Saul's knowledge, on their daring, perilous scouting expedition against the Philistines. What fighting there was in olden days over that tumbled country of hills and gorges, stretching away north to the blue mountains of Sa-maria and the summits of Ebal and Gerizim on the horizon!

There on the rocky backbone of Benjamin and

Ephraim, was Ramallah (where we had spent Sunday in the sweet orderliness of the Friends' Mission School), and Beëroth, and Bethel, and Gilgal, and Shiloh. Eastward, behind the hills, we could trace the long, vast trench of the Jordan valley running due north and south, filled with thin violet haze and terminating in a glint of the Dead Sea. Beyond that deep line of division rose the mountains of Gilead and Moab, a lofty, unbroken barrier. To the south-east we could see the red roofs of the new Jerusalem, and a few domes and minarets of the ancient city. Beyond them, in the south, was the truncated cone of the Frank Mountain, where the crusaders made their last stand against the Saracens; and the hills around Bethlehem; and a glimpse, nearer at hand, of the tall cypresses and peaceful gardens of 'Ain Karîm.

This terrestrial paradise of vision encircled us with jewel-hues and clear, exquisite outlines. Below us were the flat roofs of Nebi Samwîl, with a dog barking on every roof; the filthy courtyards and dark doorways, with a woman in one of them making bread; the ruined archways and broken cisterns with a pool of green water stagnating in one corner; peasants ploughing their stony little fields, and a string of donkeys winding up the steep path to the hill.

Here, centuries ago, Samuel called all Israel to Mizpah, and offered sacrifice before Jehovah, and judged the people. Here he inspired them with new courage and sent them down to discomfit the Philistines. Hither he came as judge and ruler of Israel, making his annual circuit between Gilgal and Bethel and Mizpah. Here he assembled the tribes again, when they were tired of his rule, and gave them a King according to their desire, even the tall warrior Saul, the son of Kish.

Do the bones of the prophet rest here or at Ramah? I do not know. But here, on this commanding peak, he began and ended his judgeship; from this aerie he looked forth upon the inheritance of the turbulent sons of Jacob; and here, if you like, to-day, a pale, clever young Mohammedan will show you what he calls the coffin of Samuel.

THE MOUNT OF OLIVES

II

THE HILL THAT JESUS LOVED

WE had seen from Mizpah the sharp ridge of the Mount of Olives, rising beyond Jerusalem. Our road thither from the camp led us around the city, past the Damascus Gate, and the royal grottoes, and Herod's Gate, and the Tower of the Storks, and St. Stephen's Gate, down into the Valley of the Brook Kidron. Here, on the west, rises the precipitous Temple Hill crowned with the wall of the city, and on the east the long ridge of Olivet.

There are several buildings on the side of the steep hill, marking supposed holy places or sacred events—the Church of the Tomb of the Virgin, the Latin Chapel of the Agony, the Greek Church of St. Mary Magdalen. On top of the ridge are the Russian Buildings, with the Chapel of the Ascension, and the Latin Buildings, with the Church of the Creed, the Church of the Paternoster, and a Carmelite Nunnery. Among the walls of these inclosures we wound our way, and at last tied our horses outside of the Russian garden. We climbed the two hundred and fourteen steps of the lofty Belvidere Tower, and found ourselves in possession of one of the great views of the world. There is Jerusalem, across the Kidron, spread out like a raised map below us. The mountains of Judah roll away north and south and east and west—the clean-cut pinnacle of Mizpah, the lofty plain of Rephaïm, the dark hills toward Hebron, the rounded top of Scopus where Titus camped with his Roman legions, the flattened peak of Frank Mountain. Bethlehem is not visible; but there is the tiny village of Bethphage, and the first roof of Bethany peeping over the ridge, and the Inn of the Good Samaritan in a red cut of the long serpentine road to Jericho. The dark range of Gilead and Moab seems like a huge wall of lapis-lazuli beyond the furrowed, wrinkled, yellowish clay-hills and the wide gray trench of the Jordan Valley, wherein the river marks its crooked path with a line of deep green. The hundreds of ridges that slope steeply down to that immense depression are touched with a thousand hues of amethystine light, and the ravines between them filled with a thousand tones of azure shadow. At the end of the valley glitter the blue waters of the Dead Sea, fifteen miles away, four thousand feet below us, yet seeming so near that we almost expect to hear the sound of its waves on the rocky shores of the Wilderness of Tekoa.

On this mount Jesus of Nazareth often walked with His disciples. On this widespread landscape His eyes rested as He spoke divinely of the invisible kingdom of peace and love and joy that shall never pass away. Over this walled city, sleeping in the sunshine, full of earthly dreams and disappointments, battlemented hearts and whited sepulchres of the spirit, He wept, and cried: "O Jerusalem, how often would I have gathered thy children together even as a hen gathereth her own brood under her wings, and ye would not!"

III

THE GARDEN OF GETHSEMANE

Come down, now, from the mount of vision to the grove of olive-trees, the Garden of Gethsemane, where Jesus used to take refuge with His friends. It lies on the eastern slope of Olivet, not far above the Valley of Kidron, over against that city-gate which was called the Beautiful, or the Golden, but which is now walled up.

The grove probably belonged to some friend of Jesus or of one of His disciples, who permitted them to make use of it for their quiet meetings. At that time, no doubt, the whole hillside was covered with olive-trees, but most of these have now disappeared. The eight aged trees that still cling to life in Gethsemane have been inclosed with a low wall and an iron railing, and the little garden that blooms around them is cared for by Franciscan monks from Italy.

The gentle, friendly Fra Giovanni, in bare sandaled feet, coarse brown robe, and broad-brimmed straw hat, is walking among the flowers. He opens the gate for us and courteously invites us in, telling us in broken French that we may pick what flowers we like. Presently I fall into discourse with him in broken Italian, telling him of my visit years ago to the cradle of his Order at Assisi, and to its most beautiful shrine at La Verna, high above the Val d'Arno. His old eyes soften into youthful brightness as he speaks of Italy. It was most beautiful, he said, *bellisima!* But he is happier here, caring for this garden, it is most holy, *santissima!*

The bronzed Mohammedan gardener, silent, patient, absorbed in his task, moves with his watering-pot among the beds, quietly refreshing the thirsty blossoms. There are wall-flowers, stocks, pansies, baby's breath, pinks, anemones of all colours, rosemary, rue, poppies—all sorts of sweet old-fashioned flowers. Among them stand the scattered venerable trees, with enormous trunks, wrinkled and contorted, eaten away by age, patched and built up with stones, protected and tended with pious care, as if they were very old people whose life must be tenderly nursed and sheltered. Their boles hardly seem to be of wood; so dark, so twisted, so furrowed are they, of an aspect so enduring that they appear to be cast in bronze or carved out of black granite. Above each of them spreads a crown of fresh foliage, delicate, abundant, shimmering softly in the sunlight and the breeze, with silken turnings of the under side of the innumerable leaves. In the centre of the garden is a kind of open flower house with a fountain of flowing water, erected in memory of a young American girl. At each corner a pair of slender cypresses lift their black-green spires against the blanched azure of the sky.

It is a place of refuge, of ineffable tranquillity, of unforgetful tenderness. The inclosure does not offend. How else could this sacred shrine of the out-of-doors be preserved? And what more fitting guardian for it than the Order of that loving Saint Francis, who called the sun and the moon his brother and his sister and preached to a joyous congregation of birds as his "little brothers of the air"? The flowers do not offend. Their antique fragrance, gracious order, familiar looks, are a symbol of what faithful memory does with the sorrows and sufferings of those who have loved us best—she treasures and transmutes them into something beautiful, she grows her sweetest flowers in the ground that tears have made holy.

It is here, in this quaint and carefully tended garden, this precious place which has been saved alike from the oblivious trampling of the crowd and from the needless imprisonment of four walls and a roof, it is here in the open air, in the calm glow of the afternoon, under the shadow of Mount Zion, that we find for the first time that which we have come so far to seek,—the soul of the Holy Land, the inward sense of the real presence of Jesus.

It is as clear and vivid as any outward experience. Why should I not speak of it as simply and candidly? Nothing that we have yet seen in Palestine, no vision of wide-spread landscape, no sight of ancient ruin or famous building or treasured relic, comes as close to our hearts as this little garden sleeping in the sun. Nothing that we have read from our Bibles in the new light of this journey has been for us so suddenly illumined, so deeply and tenderly brought home to us, as the story of Gethsemane.

Here, indeed, in the moonlit shadow of these

olives—if not of these very branches, yet of others sprung from the same immemorial stems—was endured the deepest suffering ever borne for man, the most profound sorrow of the greatest Soul that loved all human souls. It was not in the temptation in the wilderness, as Milton imagined, that the crisis of the Divine life was enacted and Paradise was regained. It was in the agony in the garden.

Here the love of life wrestled in the heart of Jesus with the purpose of sacrifice, and the anguish of that wrestling wrung the drops of blood from Him like sweat. Here, for the only time, He found the cup of sorrow and shame too bitter, and prayed the Father to take it from His lips if it were possible—possible without breaking faith, without surrendering love. For that He would not do, though His soul was exceeding sorrowful, even unto death. Here He learned the frailty of human friendship, the narrowness and dulness and coldness of the very hearts for whom He had done and suffered most, who could not even watch with Him one hour.

What infinite sense of the poverty and feebleness of mankind, the inveteracy of selfishness, the uncertainty of human impulses and aspirations and promises; what poignant questioning of the necessity, the utility of self-immolation must have tortured the soul of Jesus in that hour! It was His black hour. None can imagine the depth of that darkness but those who have themselves passed through some of its outer shadows, in the times when love seems vain, and sacrifice futile, and friendship meaningless, and life a failure, and death intolerable.

Jesus met the spirit of despair in the Garden of Gethsemane; and after that meeting, the cross had no terrors for Him, because He had already endured them; the grave no fear, because He had already conquered it. How calm and gentle was the voice with which He wakened His disciples, how firm the step with which He went to meet Judas! The bitterness of death was behind Him in the shadow of the olive-trees. The peace of Heaven shone above Him in the silent stars.

A PSALM OF SURRENDER

Mine enemies have prevailed against me, O God:
Thou hast led me deep into their ambush.

They surround me with a hedge of spears:
And the sword in my hand is broken.

My friends also have forsaken my side:
From a safe place they look upon me with pity.

My heart is like water poured upon the ground:
I have come alone to the place of surrender.

To thee, to thee only will I give up my sword:
The sword which was broken in thy service.

Thou hast required me to suffer for thy cause:
By my defeat thy will is victorious.

O my King show me thy face shining in the dark:
While I drink the loving-cup of death to thy glory.

V

AN EXCURSION TO BETHLE-HEM AND HEBRON

I

BETHLEHEM

A SPARKLING morning followed a showery
night, and all the little red and white and yellow
flowers were lifting glad faces to the sun as we took
the highroad to Bethlehem. Leaving the Jaffa Gate
on the left, we crossed the head of the deep Valley
of Hinnom, below the dirty Pool of the Sultan,
and rode up the hill on the opposite side of the
vale.

There was much rubbish and filth around us, and
the sight of the Ophthalmic Hospital of the English
Knights of Saint John, standing in the beauty of
cleanness and order beside the road, did our eyes
good. Blindness is one of the common afflictions
of the people of Palestine. Neglect and ignorance
and dirt and the plague of crawling flies spread the
germs of disease from eye to eye, and the people sub-
mit to it with pathetic and irritating fatalism. It is
hard to persuade these poor souls that the will of

Allah or Jehovah in this matter ought not to be accepted until after it has been questioned. But the light of true and humane religion is spreading a little. We rejoiced to see the reception-room of the hospital filled with all sorts and conditions of men, women and children waiting for the good physicians who save and restore sight in the name of Jesus.

To the right, a little below us, lay the ugly railway station; before us, rising gently southward, extended the elevated Plain of Rephaïm where David smote the host of the Philistines after he had heard "the sound of a going in the tops of the mulberry-trees." The red soil was cultivated in little farms and gardens. The almond-trees were in leaf; the hawthorn in blossom; the fig-trees were putting forth their tender green.

A slowly ascending road brought us to the hill of Mâr Elyâs, and the so-called Well of the Magi. Here the legend says the Wise Men halted after they had left Jerusalem, and the star reappeared to guide them on to Bethlehem. Certain it is that they must have taken this road; and certain it is that both Bethlehem and Jerusalem, hidden from each other

A Street in Bethlehem.

by the rising ground, are clearly visible to one who stands in the saddle of this hill.

There were fine views down the valleys to the east, with blue glimpses of the Dead Sea at the end of them. The supposed tomb of Rachel, a dingy little building with a white dome, interested us less than the broad lake of olive-orchards around the distant village of Beit Jâlâ, and the green fields, pastures and gardens encircling the double hill of Bethlehem, the ancient "House of Bread." There was an aspect of fertility and friendliness about the place that seemed in harmony with its name and its poetic memories.

In a walled kitchen-garden at the entrance of the town was David's Well. We felt no assurance, of course, as we looked down into it, that this was the veritable place. But at all events it served to bring back to us one of the prettiest bits of romance in the Old Testament. When the bold son of Jesse had become a chieftain of outlaws and was besieged by the Philistines in the stronghold of Adullam, his heart grew thirsty for a draught from his father's well, whose sweetness he had known as a boy. And when his three mighty men went up secretly at the risk of their lives, and broke through the host of their enemies, and brought their captain a vessel of this water, "he would not drink thereof, but poured it out unto Jehovah."

There was a division of opinion in our party in regard to this act. "It was sheer foolishness," said the Patriarch, "to waste anything that had cost so much to get. What must the three mighty men have thought when they saw that for which they had risked their lives poured out upon the ground?" "Ah, no," said the Lady. "It was the highest gratitude, because it was touched with poetry. It was the best compliment that David could have given to his friends. Some gifts are too precious to be received in any other way than this." And in my heart I knew that she was right.

Riding through the narrow streets of the town, which is inhabited almost entirely by Christians, we noted the tranquil good looks of the women, a distinct type, rather short of stature, round-faced, placid and kind of aspect. Not a few of them had blue eyes. They wore dark-blue skirts, dark-red jackets, and a white veil over their heads, but not over their faces.

Under the veil the married women wore a peculiar cap of stiff, embroidered black cloth, about six inches high, and across the front of this cap was strung their dowry of gold or silver coins. Such a dress, no doubt, was worn by the Virgin Mary, and such tranquil, friendly looks, I think, were hers, but touched with a rarer light of beauty shining from a secret source within.

A crowd of little boys and girls just released from school for their recess shouted and laughed and chased one another, pausing for a moment in round-eyed wonder when I pointed my camera at them. Donkeys and camels and sheep made our passage through the town slow, and gave us occasion to look to our horses' footing. At one corner a great white sow ran out of an alley-way, followed by a twinkling litter of pink pigs. In the market-place we left our horses in the shadow of the monastery wall and entered, by a low door, the lofty, bare Church of the Nativity.

The long rows of immense marble pillars had some faded remains of painting on them. There were a few battered fragments of mosaic in the clerestory, dimly glittering. But the general effect of the whitewashed walls, the ancient brown beams and rafters of the roof, the large, empty space, was one of extreme simplicity.

When we came into the choir and apse we found ourselves in the midst of complexity. The ownership of the different altars with their gilt ornaments, of the swinging lamps, of the separate doorways of the Greeks and the Armenians and the Latins, was bewildering. Dark, winding steps, slippery with the drippings from many candles, led us down into the Grotto of the Nativity. It was a cavern perhaps forty feet long and ten feet wide, lit by thirty pendent lamps (Greek, Armenian and Latin): marble floor and walls hung with draperies; a silver star in the pavement before the altar to mark the spot where Christ was born; a marble manger in the corner to mark the cradle in which Christ was laid; a never-ceasing stream of poor pilgrims, who come kneeling, and kissing the star and the stones and the altar for Christ's sake.

We paused for a while, after we had come up, to ask ourselves whether what we had seen was in any

The Market-place, Bethlehem.

way credible. Yes, credible, but not convincing. No doubt the ancient Khân of Bethlehem must have been somewhere near this spot, in the vicinity of the market-place of the town. No doubt it was the custom, when there were natural hollows or artificial grottos in the rock near such an inn, to use them as shelters and stalls for the cattle. It is quite possible, it is even probable, that this may have been one of the shallow caverns used for such a purpose. If so, there is no reason to deny that this may be the place of the wondrous birth, where, as the old French *Noel* has it:

> "*Dieu parmy les pastoreaux,*
> *Sous la crêche des toreaux,*
> *Dans les champs a voulu naistre;*
> *Et non parmy les arroys*
> *Des grands princes et des roys,—*
> *Lui des plus grands roys le maistre.*"

But to the eye, at least, there is no reminder of the scene of the Nativity in this close and stifling chapel, hung with costly silks and embroideries, glittering with rich lamps, filled with the smoke of incense and waxen tapers. And to the heart there is little suggestion of the lonely night when Joseph found a humble refuge here for his young bride to wait in darkness, pain and hope for her hour to come.

In the church above, the Latins and Armenians and Greeks guard their privileges and prerogatives jealously. There have been fights here about the driving of a nail, the hanging of a picture, the sweeping of a bit of the floor. The Crimean War began in a quarrel between the Greeks and the Latins, and a mob-struggle in the Church of the Nativity. Underneath the floor, to the north of the Grotto of the Nativity, is the cave in which Saint Jerome lived peaceably for many years, translating the Bible into Latin. That was better than fighting.

II

ON THE ROAD TO HEBRON

We ate our lunch at Bethlehem in a curiosity-shop. The table was spread at the back of the room by the open window. All around us were hanging innumerable chaplets and rosaries of mother-of-pearl, of carnelian, of carved olive-stones, of glass beads; trinkets and souvenirs of all imaginable kinds, tiny sheep-bells and inlaid boxes and carved fans filled the cases and cabinets. Through the window came the noise of people busy at Bethlehem's chief industry, the cutting and polishing of mother-of-pearl for mementoes. The jingling bells of our pack-train, passing the open door, reminded us that our camp was to be pitched miles away on the road to Hebron.

We called for the horses and rode on through the town. Very beautiful and peaceful was the view from the southern hill, looking down upon the pastures of Bethlehem where "shepherds watched their flocks by night," and the field of Boaz where Ruth followed the reapers among the corn.

Down dale and up hill we journeyed; bright green of almond-trees, dark green of carob-trees, snowy blossoms of apricot-trees, rosy blossoms of peach-trees, argent verdure of olive-trees, adorning the valleys. Then out over the wilder, rockier heights; and past the great empty Pools of Solomon, lying at the head of the Wâdi Artâs, watched by a square ruined castle; and up the winding road and along the lofty flower-sprinkled ridges; and at last we came to our tents, pitched in the wide, green Wâdi el-'Arrûb, beside the bridge.

Springs gushed out of the hillside here and ran down in a little laughing brook through lawns full of tiny pink and white daisies, and broad fields of tangled weeds and flowers, red anemones, blue iris, purple mallows, scarlet adonis, with here and there a strip of cultivated ground shimmering with silky leeks or dotted with young cucumbers. There was a broken aqueduct cut in the rock at the side of the valley, and the brook slipped by a large ruined reservoir.

"George," said I to the Bethlehemite, as he sat meditating on the edge of the dry pool, "what do you think of this valley?"

"I think," said George, "that if I had a few thousand dollars to buy the land, with all this runaway water I could make it blossom like a peach-tree."

The cold, green sunset behind the western hills darkened into night. The air grew chilly, dropping nearly to the point of frost. We missed the blazing camp-fire of the Canadian forests, and went to bed early, tucking in the hot-water bags at our feet and piling on the blankets and rugs. All through the night we could hear the passers-by shouting and singing along the Hebron road. There was one unknown traveller whose high-pitched, quavering Arab song rose far away, and grew louder as he approached, and passed us in a whirlwind of lugubrious music, and tapered slowly off into distance and silence—a chant a mile long.

The morning broke through flying clouds, with a bitter, wet, west wind rasping the bleak highlands. There were spiteful showers with intervals of mocking sunshine; it was a mischievous and prankish bit of weather, no day for riding. But the Lady was indomitable, so we left the Patriarch in his tent, wrapped ourselves in garments of mackintosh and took the road again.

The country, at first, was wild and barren, a wilderness of rocks and thorn bushes and stunted scrub oaks. Now and then a Greek partridge, in its beautiful plumage of fawn-gray, marked with red and black about the head, clucked like a hen on the stony hillside, or whirred away in low, straight flight over the bushes. Flocks of black and brown goats, with pendulous ears, skipped up and down the steep ridges, standing up on their hind legs to browse the foliage of the little oak shrubs, or showing themselves off in a butting-match on top of a big rock. Marching on the highroad they seemed sedate, despondent, pattering along soberly with flapping ears. In the midst of one flock I saw a fierce-looking tattered pastor tenderly carrying a little black kid in his bosom—as tenderly as if it were a lamb. It seemed like an illustration of a picture that I saw long ago in the Catacombs, in which the infant church of Christ silently expressed the richness of her love, the breadth of her hope:

> "On those walls subterranean, where she hid
> Her head 'mid ignominy, death and tombs,
> She her Good Shepherd's hasty image drew—
> And on His shoulders, not a lamb, a kid."

As we drew nearer to Hebron the region appeared more fertile, and the landscape smiled a little under the gleams of wintry sunshine. There were many vineyards; in most of them the vines trailed along the ground, but in some they were propped up on sticks, like old men leaning on crutches. Almond and apricot-trees flourished. The mulberries, the olives, the sycamores were abundant. Peasants were ploughing the fields with their crooked sticks shod with a long iron point. When a man puts his hand to such a plough he dares not look back, else it will surely go aside. It makes a scratch, not a furrow. (I saw a man in the hospital at Nazareth who had his thigh pierced clear through by one of these dagger-like iron plough points.)

Children were gathering roots and thorn branches for firewood. Women were carrying huge bundles on their heads. Donkey-boys were urging their heavy-laden animals along the road, and cameleers led their deliberate strings of ungainly beasts by a rope or a light chain reaching from one nodding head to another.

A camel's load never looks as large as a donkey's, but no doubt he often finds it heavy, and he always looks displeased with it. There is something about the droop of a camel's lower lip which seems to express unalterable disgust with the universe. But the rest of the world around Hebron appeared to be reasonably happy. In spite of weather and poverty and hard work the ploughmen sang in the fields, the children skipped and whistled at their tasks, the passers-by on the road shouted greetings to the labourers in the gardens and vineyards. Somewhere round about here is supposed to lie the Valley of Eshcol from which the Hebrew spies brought back the monstrous bunch of grapes, a cluster that reached from the height of a man's shoulder to the ground.

III

THE TENTING-GROUND OF ABRAHAM

HEBRON lies three thousand feet above the sea, and is one of the ancient market-places and shrines of the world. From time immemorial it has been a holy town, a busy town, and a turbulent town. The Hittites and the Amorites dwelt here, and Abraham, a nomadic shepherd whose tents followed his flocks over the land of Canaan, bought here his only piece of real estate, the field and cave of Machpelah. He bought it for a tomb,—even a nomad wishes to rest quietly in death,—and here he and his wife Sarah, and his children Isaac and Rebekah, and his grandchildren Jacob and Leah were buried.

The modern town has about twenty thousand inhabitants, chiefly Mohammedans of a fanatical temper, and is incredibly dirty. We passed the muddy pool by which King David, when he was reigning here, hanged the murderers of Ishbosheth. We climbed the crooked streets to the Mosque which covers the supposed site of the cave of Machpelah. But we did not see the tomb of Abraham, for no "infidel" is allowed to pass beyond the seventh step in the flight of stairs which leads up to the doorway.

As we went down through the narrow, dark, crowded Bazaar a violent storm of hail broke over the city, pelting into the little open shops and covering the streets half an inch deep with snowy sand and pebbles of ice. The tempest was a rude joke, which seemed to surprise the surly crowd into a good humour. We laughed with the Moslems as we took shelter together from our common misery under a stone archway.

After the storm had passed we ate our midday

meal on a housetop, which a friend of the dragoman
put at our disposal, and rode out in the afternoon to
the Oak of Abraham on the hill of Mamre. The
tree is an immense, battered veteran, with a trunk
ten feet in diameter, and wide-flung, knotted arms
which still bear a few leaves and acorns. It has been
inclosed with a railing, patched up with masonry,
partially protected by a roof. The Russian monks
who live near by have given it pious care, yet its inevitable end is surely near.

The death of a great sheltering tree has a kind of
dumb pathos. It seems like the passing away of
something beneficent and helpless, something that
was able to shield others but not itself.

On this hill, under the oaks of Mamre, Abraham's
tents were pitched many a year, and here he enter-
tained the three angels unawares, and Sarah made
pancakes for them, and listened behind the tent-flap
while they were talking with her husband, and
laughed at what they said. This may not be the
very tree that flung its shadow over the tent, but
no doubt it is a son or a grandson of that tree, and
the acorns that still fall from it may be the seeds of

other oaks to shelter future generations of pilgrims; and so throughout the world, the ancient covenant of friendship is unbroken, and man remains a grateful lover of the big, kind trees.

We got home to our camp in the green meadow of the springs late in the afternoon, and on the third day we rode back to Jerusalem, and pitched the tents in a new place, on a hill opposite the Jaffa Gate, with a splendid view of the Valley of Hinnom, the Tower of David, and the western wall of the city.

A PSALM OF FRIENDLY TREES

I will sing of the bounty of the big trees,
They are the green tents of the Almighty,
He hath set them up for comfort and for shelter.

Their cords hath he knotted in the earth,
He hath driven their stakes securely,
Their roots take hold of the rocks like iron.

He sendeth into their bodies the sap of life,
They lift themselves lightly towards the heavens.
They rejoice in the broadening of their branches.

Their leaves drink in the sunlight and the air,
They talk softly together when the breeze bloweth,
Their shadow in the noonday is full of coolness.

The tall palm-trees of the plain are rich in fruit,
While the fruit ripeneth the flower unfoldeth,
The beauty of their crown is renewed on high forever.

The cedars of Lebanon are fed by the snow,
Afar on the mountain they grow like giants,
In their layers of shade a thousand years are sighing.

How fair are the trees that befriend the home of man,
The oak, and the terebinth, and the sycamore,
The fruitful fig-tree and the silvery olive.

In them the Lord is loving to his little birds,—
The linnets and the finches and the nightingales,—
They people his pavilions with nests and with music.

The cattle are very glad of a great tree,
They chew the cud beneath it while the sun is
    burning,
There also the panting sheep lie down around their
    shepherd.

He that planteth a tree is a servant of God,
He provideth a kindness for many generations,
And faces that he hath not seen shall bless him.

Lord, when my spirit shall return to thee,
At the foot of a friendly tree let my body be buried,
That this dust may rise and rejoice among the
    branches.

VI

THE TEMPLE AND THE SEPULCHRE

I

THE DOME OF THE ROCK

THERE is an upward impulse in man that draws him to a hilltop for his place of devotion and sanctuary of ascending thoughts. The purer air, the wider outlook, the sense of freedom and elevation, help to release his spirit from the weight that bends his forehead to the dust. A traveller in Palestine, if he had wings, could easily pass through the whole land by short flights from the summit of one holy hill to another, and look down from a series of mountain-altars upon the wrinkled map of sacred history without once descending into the valley or toiling over the plain. But since there are no wings provided in the human outfit, our journey from shrine to shrine must follow the common way of men,—which is also a symbol,—the path of up-and-down, and many windings, and weary steps.

The oldest of the shrines of Jerusalem is the threshing-floor of Araunah the Jebusite, which David bought from him in order that it might be made the site of the Temple of Jehovah. No doubt the King knew of the traditions which connected the place with ancient and famous rites of worship. But I think he was moved also by the commanding beauty of the situation, on the very summit of Mount Moriah, looking down into the deep Valley of the Kidron.

Our way to this venerable and sacred hill leads through the crooked duskiness of David Street, and across the half-filled depression of the Tyropœon Valley which divides the city, and up through the dim, deserted Bazaar of the Cotton Merchants, and so through the central western gate of the Haram-esh-Sherîf, "the Noble Sanctuary."

This is a great inclosure, clean, spacious, airy, a place of refuge from the foul confusion of the city streets. The wall that shuts us in is almost a mile long, and within this open space, which makes an immediate effect of breadth and tranquil order, are some of the most sacred buildings of Islam and some of the most significant landmarks of Christianity.

Slender and graceful arcades are outlined against the clear, blue sky: little domes are poised over praying-places and fountains of ablution: wide and easy flights of steps lead from one level to another, in this park of prayer.

At the southern end, beyond the tall cypresses and the plashing fountain fed from Solomon's Pools, stands the long Mosque el-Aksa: to Mohammedans, the place to which Allah brought their prophet from Mecca in one night; to Christians, the Basilica which the Emperor Justinian erected in honor of the Virgin Mary. At the northern end rises the ancient wall of the Castle of Antonia, from whose steps Saint Paul, protected by the Roman captain, spoke his defence to the Jerusalem mob. The steps, hewn partly in the solid rock, are still visible; but the site of the castle is occupied by the Turkish barracks, beside which the tallest minaret of the Haram lifts its covered gallery high above the corner of the great wall.

Yonder to the east is the Golden Gate, above the steep Valley of Jehoshaphat. It is closed with great stones; because the Moslem tradition says that some Friday a Christian conqueror will enter Jerusalem by that gate. Not far away we see the column in the wall from which the Mohammedans believe a slender rope, or perhaps a naked sword, will be stretched, in the judgment day, to the Mount of Olives opposite. This, according to them, will be the bridge over which all human souls must walk, while Christ sits at one end, Mohammed at the other, watching and judging. The righteous, upheld by angels, will pass safely; the wicked, heavy with unbalanced sins, will fall.

Dominating all these wide-spread relics and shrines, in the centre of the inclosure, on a raised platform approached through delicate arcades, stands the great Dome of the Rock, built by Abd-el-Melik in 688 A.D., on the site of the Jewish Temple. The exterior of the vast octagon, with its lower half cased in marble and its upper half incrusted with Persian tiles of blue and green, its broad, round lantern and swelling black dome surmounted by a glittering crescent, is bathed in full sunlight; serene, proud, eloquent of a certain splendid simplicity. Within, the light filters dimly through windows of stained glass and falls on marble columns, bronzed beams, mosaic walls, screens of wrought iron and carved wood.

We walk as if through an interlaced forest and undergrowth of rich entangled colours. It all seems vi-
sionary, unreal, fantastic, until we climb the bench
by the end of the inner screen and look upon the
Rock over which the Dome is built.

This is the real thing,—a plain gray limestone rock,
level and fairly smooth, the unchanged summit of
Mount Moriah. Here the priest-king Melchizedek
offered sacrifice. Here Abraham, in the cruel fervour
of his faith, was about to slay his only son Isaac because he thought it would please Jehovah. Here
Araunah the Jebusite threshed his corn on the
smooth rock and winnowed it in the winds of the
hilltop, until King David stepped over from Mount
Zion, and bought the threshing-floor and the oxen of
him for fifty shekels of silver, and built in this place
an altar to the Lord. Here Solomon erected his splendid Temple and the Chaldeans burned it. Here
Zerubbabel built the second Temple after the return
of the Jews from exile, and Antiochus Epiphanes des-
ecrated it, and Herod burned part of it and pulled
down the rest. Here Herod built the third Temple,
larger and more magnificent than the first, and the

111

soldiers of the Emperor Titus burned it. Here the
Emperor Hadrian built a temple to Jupiter and
himself, and some one, perhaps the Christians,
burned it. Here Mohammed came to pray, declaring that one prayer here was worth a thousand elsewhere. Here the Caliph Omar built a little wooden
mosque, and the Caliph Abd-el-Melik replaced it
with this great one of marble, and the Crusaders
changed it into a Christian temple, and Saladin
changed it back again into a mosque.

This Haram-esh-Sherîf is the second holiest place
in the Moslem world. Hither come the Mohammedan pilgrims by thousands, for the sake of Mohammed. Hither come the Christian pilgrims by thousands, for the sake of Him who said: "Neither in
this mountain nor in Jerusalem shall ye worship the
Father." Hither the Jewish pilgrims never come,
for fear their feet may unwittingly tread upon "the
Holy of Holies," and defile it; but they creep outside
of the great inclosure, in the gloomy trench beside
the foundation stones of the wall, mourning and lamenting for the majesty that is departed and the
Temple that is ground to powder.

But amid all these changes and perturbations, here stands the good old limestone rock, the threshing-floor of Araunah, the capstone of the hill, waiting for the sun to shine and the dews to fall on it once more, as they did when the foundations of the earth were laid.

The legend says that you can hear the waters of the flood roaring in an abyss underneath the rock. I laid my ear against the rugged stone and listened. What sound? Was it the voice of turbulent centuries and the lapsing tides of men?

II

GOLGOTHA

" WE ought to go again to the Church of the Holy Sepulchre," said the Lady in a voice of dutiful reminder, "we have not half seen it." So we went down to the heart of Jerusalem and entered the labyrinthine shrine.

The motley crowd in the paved quadrangle in front of the double-arched doorway were buying and selling, bickering and chaffering and chattering as

113

usual. Within the portal, on a slightly raised platform to the left, the Turkish guardians of the holy
places and keepers of the peace between Christians
were seated among their rugs and cushions, impassive, indolent, dignified, drinking their coffee or
smoking their tobacco, conversing gravely or count-
ing the amber beads of their comboloios. The Sultan
owns the Holy Sepulchre; but he is a liberal host
and permits all factions of Christendom to visit it
and celebrate their rites in turn, provided only they
do not beat or kill one another in their devotions.
We saw his silent sentinels of tolerance scattered
in every part of the vast, confused edifice.

The interior was dim and shadowy. Opposite the
entrance was the Stone of Unction, a marble slab on
which it is said the body of Christ was anointed
when it was taken down from the cross. Pilgrim
after pilgrim came kneeling to this stone, and bending to kiss it, beneath the Latin, Greek, Armenian
and Coptic lamps which hang above it by silver
chains.

The Chapel of the Crucifixion was on our right,
above us, in the second story of the church. We

climbed the steep flight of stairs and stood in a little room, close, obscure, crowded with lamps and icons and candelabra, incrusted with ornaments of gold and silver, full of strange odours and glimmerings of mystic light. There, they told us, in front of that rich altar was the silver star which marked the place in the rock where the Holy Cross stood. And on either side of it were the sockets which received the crosses of the two thieves. And a few feet away, covered by a brass slide, was the cleft in the rock which was made by the earthquake. It was lined with slabs of reddish marble and looked nearly a foot deep.

Priests in black robes and tall, cylindrical hats, and others with brown robes, rope girdles and tonsured heads, were coming and going around us. Pilgrims were climbing and descending the stairs, kneeling and murmuring unintelligible devotions, kissing the star and the cleft in the rock and the icons. Underneath us, though we were supposed to stand on the hill called Golgotha, were the offices of the Greek clergy and the Chapel of Adam.

We went around from chapel to chapel; into the

opulent Greek cathedral where they show the "Centre of the World"; into the bare little Chapel of the Syrians where they show the tombs of Nicodemus and Joseph of Arimathæa; into the Chapel of the Apparition where the Franciscans say that Christ appeared to His mother after the resurrection. There was sweet singing in this chapel and a fragrant smell of incense. We went into the Chapel of Saint Helena, underground, which belongs to the Greeks; into the Chapel of the Parting of the Raiment which belongs to the Armenians. We were impartial in our visitation, but we did not have time to see the Abyssinian Chapel, the Coptic Chapel of Saint Michael, nor the Church of Abraham where the Anglicans are allowed to celebrate the eucharist twice a month.

The centre of all this maze of creeds, ceremonies and devotions is the Chapel of the Holy Sepulchre, a little edifice of precious marbles, carved and gilded, standing beneath the great dome of the church, in the middle of a rotunda surrounded by marble pillars. We bought and lighted our waxen tapers and waited for a lull in the stream of pilgrims to enter the shrine. First we stood in the vestibule with its tall candelabra; then in the Angels' Chapel, with its fifteen swinging lamps, making darkness visible; then, stooping through a low doorway, we came into the tiny chamber, six feet square, which is said to contain the rock-hewn tomb in which the Saviour of the World was buried.

Mass is celebrated here daily by different Christian sects. Pilgrims, rich and poor, come hither from all parts of the habitable globe. They kneel beneath the three-and-forty pendent lamps of gold and silver. They kiss the worn slab of marble which covers the tombstone, some of them smiling with joy, some of them weeping bitterly, some of them with quiet, business-like devotion as if they were performing a duty. The priest of their faith blesses them, sprinkles the relics which they lay on the altar with holy water, and one by one the pilgrims retire backward through the low portal.

I saw a Russian peasant, sad-eyed, wrinkled, bent with many sorrows, lay his cheek silently on the tombstone with a look on his face as if he were a child leaning against his mother's breast. I saw a little barefoot boy of Jerusalem, with big, serious eyes, come quickly in, and try to kiss the stone; but it was too high for him, so he kissed his hand and laid it upon the altar. I saw a young nun, hardly more than a girl, slender, pale, dark-eyed, with a noble Italian face, shaken with sobs, the tears running down her cheeks, as she bent to touch her lips to the resting-place of the Friend of Sinners.

This, then, is the way in which the craving for penitence, for reverence, for devotion, for some utterance of the nameless thirst and passion of the soul leads these pilgrims. This is the form in which the divine mystery of sacrificial sorrow and death appeals to them, speaks to their hearts and comforts them.

Could any Christian of whatever creed, could any son of woman with a heart to feel the trouble and longing of humanity, turn his back upon that altar? Must I not go away from that mysterious little room as the others had gone, with my face toward the stone of remembrance, stooping through the lowly door?

And yet—and yet in my deepest heart I was

thirsty for the open air, the blue sky, the pure sunlight, the tranquillity of large and silent spaces.

The Lady went with me across the crowded quadrangle into the cool, clean, quiet German Church of the Redeemer. We climbed to the top of the lofty bell tower.

Jerusalem lay at our feet, with its network of streets and lanes, archways and convent walls, domes small and great—the black Dome of the Rock in the centre of its wide inclosure, the red dome and the green dome of the Jewish synagogues on Mount Zion, the seven gilded domes of the Russian Church of Saint Mary Magdalen, a hundred tiny domes of dwelling-houses, and right in front of us the yellow dome of the Greek "Centre of the World" and the black dome of the Holy Sepulchre.

The quadrangle was still full of people buying and selling, but the murmur of their voices was faint and far away, less loud than the twittering of the thousands of swallows that soared and circled, with glistening of innumerable blue-black wings and soft sheen of white breasts, in the tender light of sunset above the façade of the gray old church.

119

Westward the long ridge of Olivet was bathed in the rays of the declining sun.

Northward, beyond the city-gate, the light fell softly on a little rocky hill, shaped like a skull, the ancient place of stoning for those whom the cruel city had despised and rejected and cast out. At the foot of that eminence there is a quiet garden and a tomb hewn in the rock. Rosemary and rue grow there, roses and lilies; birds sing among the trees. Is not that little rounded hill, still touched with the free light of heaven, still commanding a clear outlook over the city to the Mount of Olives—is not that the true Golgotha, where Christ was lifted up?

As we were thinking of this we saw a man come out on the roof of the Greek "Centre of the World," and climb by a ladder up the side of the huge dome. He went slowly and carefully, yet with confidence, as if the task were familiar. He carried a lantern in one hand. He was going to the top of the dome to light up the great cross for the night. We spoke no word, but each knew the thought that was in the other's heart.

THE SEPULCHRE

Wherever the crucifixion took place, it was surely in the open air, beneath the wide sky, and the cross that stood on Golgotha has become the light at the centre of the world's night.

A PSALM OF THE UNSEEN ALTAR

Man the maker of cities is also a builder of altars:
Among his habitations he setteth tables for his god.

He bringeth the beauty of the rocks to enrich them:
Marble and alabaster, porphyry, jasper and jade.

He cometh with costly gifts to offer an oblation:
He would buy favour with the fairest of his flock.

Around the many altars I hear strange music arising:
Loud lamentations and shouting and singing and
    sighs.

I perceive also the pain and terror of their sacrifices:
I see the white marble wet with tears and with blood.

Then I said, These are the altars of ignorance:
Yet they are built by thy children, O God, who know
    thee not.

Surely thou wilt have pity upon them and lead them:
Hast thou not prepared for them a table of peace?

*Then the Lord mercifully sent his angel forth to lead
   me:*
*He led me through the temples, the holy place
   that is hidden.*

*Lo, there are multitudes kneeling in the silence of
   the spirit:*
*They are kneeling at the unseen altar of the lowly
   heart.*

*Here is plentiful forgiveness for the souls that are
   forgiving:*
*And the joy of life is given unto all who long to
   give.*

*Here a Father's hand upholdeth all who bear each
   other's burdens:*
*And the benediction falleth upon all who pray
   in love.*

*Surely this is the altar where the penitent find
   pardon:*
*And the priest who hath blessed it forever is the
   Holy One of God.*

VII

JERICHO AND JORDAN

I

"GOING DOWN TO JERICHO"

IN the memory of every visitor to Jerusalem the excursion to Jericho is a vivid point. For this is the one trip which everybody makes, and it is a convention of the route to regard it as a perilous and exciting adventure. Perhaps it is partly this flavour of a not-too-dangerous danger, this shivering charm of a hazard to be taken without too much risk, that attracts the average tourist, prudently romantic, to make the journey to the lowest inhabited town in the world.

Jericho has always had an ill name. Weak walls, weak hearts, weak morals were its early marks. Sweltering on the rich plain of the lower Jordan, eight hundred feet below the sea, at the entrance of the two chief passes into the Judean highlands, it was too indolent or cowardly to maintain its own importance. Stanley called it "the key of Palestine"; but it was only a latch which any bold invader could lift. The people of Jericho were famous for light fingers and lively feet, great robbers and runners-away. Joshua blotted the city out with a curse; five centuries later Hiel the Bethelite rebuilt it with the bloody sacrifice of his two sons. Antony gave it to Cleopatra, and Herod bought it from her for a winter palace, where he died. Nothing fine or brave, so far as I can remember, is written of any of its inhabitants, except the good deed of Rahab, a harlot, and the honest conduct of Zacchæus, a publican. To this day, at the *tables d'hôte* of Jerusalem the name of Jericho stirs up a little whirlwind of bad stories and warnings.

Last night we were dining with friends at one of the hotels, and the usual topic came up for discussion. Imagine what followed.

"That Jericho road is positively frightful," says a British female tourist in lace cap, lilac ribbons and a maroon poplin dress, "the heat is most extr'or-dinary!"

"No food fit to eat at the hotel," grumbles her husband, a rosy, bald-headed man in plaid knick-erbockers, "no bottled beer; beastly little hole!"

"A voyage of the most fatiguing, of the most perilous, I assure you," says a little Frenchman with a forked beard. "But I rejoice myself of the adventure, of the romance accomplished."

"I want to know," piped a lady in a green shirt-waist from Andover, Mass., "is there really and truly any danger?"

"I guess not for us," answers the dominating voice of the conductor of her party. "There's always a bunch of robbers on that road, but I have hired the biggest man of the bunch to take care of us. Just wait till you see that dandy Sheikh in his best clothes; he looks like a museum of old weapons."

"Have you heard," interposed a lady-like clergy-man on the other side of the table, with gold-rimmed spectacles gleaming above his high, black waistcoat, "what happened on the Jericho road, week before last? An English gentleman, of very good family, imprudently taking a short cut, became separated from his companions. The Bedouins fell upon him, beat him quite painfully, deprived him of his watch and several necessary garments, and left him prostrate upon the earth, in an embarrassingly denuded condition Just fancy! Was it not perfectly shock-ing?" (The clergyman's voice was full of delicious horror.) "But, after all," he resumed with a beam-ing smile, "it was most scriptural, you know, quite like a Providential confirmation of Holy Writ!"

"Most unpleasant for the Englishman," growls the man in knickerbockers. "But what can you expect under this rotten Turkish government?"

"I know a story about Jericho," begins a gentle-man from Colorado, with a hay-coloured moustache and a droop in his left eyelid—and then follows a series of tales about that ill-reputed town and the road thither, which leave the lady in the lace cap gasping, and the man with the forked beard visibly swelling with pride at having made the journey, and the little woman in the green shirt-waist quivering with exquisite fears and mentally clinging with both arms to the personal conductor of her party, who looks becomingly virile, and exchanges a surrepti-tious wink with the gentleman from Colorado.

Of course, I am not willing to make an affidavit to the correctness of every word in this conversation; but I can testify that it fairly represents the *Jericho-*

motif as you may hear it played almost any night in the Jerusalem hotels. It sounded to us partly like an echo of ancient legends kept alive by dragomans and officials for purposes of revenue, and partly like an outcrop of the hysterical habit in people who travel in flocks and do nothing without much palaver. In our quiet camp, George the Bethlehemite assured us that the sheikhs were "humbugs," and an escort of soldiers a nuisance. So we placidly made our preparations to ride on the morrow, with no other safeguards than our friendly dispositions and a couple of excellent American revolvers.

But it was no brief *Ausflug* to Jericho and return that we had before us: it was the beginning of a long and steady ride, weeks in the saddle, from six to nine hours a day.

Imagine us then, morning after morning, mounting somewhere between six and eight o'clock, according to the weather and the length of the journey, and jingling out of camp, followed at a discreet distance by Youssouf on his white pony with the luncheon, and Faris on his tiny donkey, Tiddlywinks. About noon, sometimes a little earlier,

131

sometimes a little later, the white pony catches up with us, and the tent and the rugs are spread for the midday meal and the *siesta*. It may be in our dreams, or while the Lady is reading from some pleasant book, or while the smoke of the afternoon pipe of peace is ascending, that we hear the musical bells of our long baggage-train go by us on the way to our night-quarters.

The evening ride is always shorter than the morning, sometimes only an hour or two in the saddle; and at the end of it there is the surprise of a new camp ground, the comfortable tents, the refreshing bath tub, the quiet dinner by sunset-glow or candle-light. Then a bit of friendly talk over the walnuts and the "Treasure of Zion"; a cup of fragrant Turkish coffee; and George enters the door of the tent to report on the condition of things in general, and to discuss the plan of the next day's journey.

II

THE GOOD SAMARITAN'S ROAD

It is strange how every day, no matter in what mood of merry jesting or practical modernity we set out, an hour of riding in the open air brings us back to the mystical charm of the Holy Land and beneath the spell of its memories and dreams. The wild hillsides, the flowers of the field, the shimmering olive-groves, the brown villages, the crumbling ruins, the deep-blue sky, subdue us to themselves and speak to us "rememberable things."

We pass down the Valley of the Brook Kidron, where no water ever flows; and through the crowd of beggars and loiterers and pilgrims at the cross-roads; and up over the shoulder of the Mount of Olives, past the wide-spread Jewish burying-ground, where we take our last look at the towers and domes and minarets and walls of Jerusalem. The road descends gently, on the other side of the hill, to Bethany, a disconsolate group of hovels. The sweet home of Mary and Martha is gone. It is a waste of time to look at the uncertain ruins which are shown

here as sacred sites. Look rather at the broad landscape eastward and southward, the luminous blue
sky, the joyful little flowers on the rocky slopes,—
these are unchanged.

Not far beyond Bethany, the road begins to drop,
with great windings, into a deep, desolate valley,
crowded with pilgrims afoot and on donkey-back
and in ramshackle carriages,—Russians and Greeks
returning from their sacred bath in the Jordan.
Here and there, at first, we can see a shepherd with
his flock upon the haggard hillside.

> "As for the grass, it grew as scant as hair
>   In leprosy."

Once the Patriarch and I, scrambling on foot
down a short-cut, think we see a Bedouin waiting for
us behind a rock, with his long gun over his shoulder; but it turns out to be only a brown little peasant
girl, ragged and smiling, watching her score of lop-
eared goats.

As the valley descends the landscape becomes
more and more arid and stricken. The heat broods
over it like a disease.

"I think I never saw
Such starved, ignoble nature; nothing throve;
For flowers—as well expect a cedar grove!"

We might be on the way with Childe Roland to the Dark Tower. But instead we come, about noon, through a savage glen beset with blood-red rocks and honeycombed with black caves on the other side of the ravine, to the so-called "Inn of the Good Samaritan."

The local colour of the parable surrounds us. Here is a fitting scene for such a drama of lawless violence, cowardly piety, and unconventional mercy. In these caverns robbers could hide securely. On this wild road their victim might lie and bleed to death. By these paths across the glen the priest and the Levite could "pass by on the other side," discreetly turning their heads away from any interruption to their selfish duties. And in some such wayside khân as this, standing like a lonely fortress among the sun-baked hills, the friendly half-heathen from Samaria could safely leave the stranger whom he had rescued, provided he paid at least a part of his lodging in advance.

135

We eat our luncheon in one of the three big, disorderly rooms of the inn, and go on, in the cool of the afternoon, toward Jericho. The road still descends steeply, among ragged and wrinkled hills. On our left we look down into the Wâdi el-Kelt, a gloomy gorge five or six hundred feet deep, with a stream of living water singing between its prison walls. Tradition calls this the Brook Cherith, where Elijah hid himself from Ahab, and was fed by Arabs of a tribe called "the Ravens." But the prophet's hiding-place was certainly on the other side of the Jordan, and this Wâdi is probably the Valley of Achor, spoken of in the Book of Joshua. On the opposite side of the cañon, half-way down the face of the precipice, clings the monastery of Saint George, one of the pious penitentiaries to which the Greek Church assigns unruly and criminal monks.

As we emerge from the narrow valley a great view opens before us: to the right, the blue waters of the Dead Sea, like a mirror of burnished steel; in front, the immense plain of the Jordan, with the dark-green ribbon of the river-jungle winding through its length and the purple mountains of Gilead and

Great Monastery of St. George.

Moab towering beyond it; to the left, the furrowed gray and yellow ridges and peaks of the northern "wilderness" of Judea, the wild country into which Jesus retired alone after the baptism by John in the Jordan.

One of these peaks, the Quarantana, is supposed to be the "high mountain" from which the Tempter showed Jesus the "kingdoms of the world." In the foreground of that view, sweeping from the snowy summits of Hermon in the north, past the Greek cities of Pella and Scythopolis, down the vast valley with its wealth of palms and balsams, must have stood the Roman city of Jericho, with its imperial farms and the palaces, baths and theatres of Herod the Great,—a visible image of what Christ might have won for Himself if He had yielded to the temptation and turned from the pathway of spiritual light to follow the shadows of earthly power and glory.

Herod's Jericho has vanished; there is nothing left of it but the outline of one of the great pools which he built to irrigate his gardens. The modern Jericho is an unhappy little adobe village, lying a mile or so farther to the east. A mile to the north, near a copious fountain of pure water, called the Sultan's Spring, is the site of the oldest Jericho, which Joshua conquered and Hiel rebuilt. The spring, which is probably the same that Elisha cleansed with salt (II Kings ii: 19–22), sends forth a merry stream to turn a mill and irrigate a group of gardens full of oranges, figs, bananas, grapes, feathery bamboos and rosy oleanders. But the ancient city is buried under a great mound of earth, which the German *Palästina-Verein* is now excavating.

As we come up to the mound I pull out my little camera and prepare to take a picture of the hundred or so dusty Arabs—men, women and children—who are at work in the trenches. A German *gelehrter* in a very excited state rushes up to me and calls upon me to halt, in the name of the Emperor. The taking of pictures by persons not imperially authorised is *streng verboten*. He is evidently prepared to be abusive, if not actually violent, until I assure him, in the best German that I can command, that I have no political or archæological intentions, and that if the photographing of his picturesque work-people to him displeasing is, I will my camera immediately in its pocket put. This mollifies him, and he politely shows us what he is doing.

A number of ruined houses, and a sort of central temple, with a rude flight of steps leading up to it, have been discovered. A portion of what seems to be the city-wall has just been laid bare. If there are any inscriptions or relics of any value they are kept secret; but there is plenty of broken pottery of a common kind. It is all very poor and beggarly looking; no carving nor even any hewn stones. The buildings seem to be of rubble, and "the walls of Jericho" are little better than the stone fences on a Connecticut farm. No wonder they fell down at the blast of Joshua's rams' horns and the rush of his fierce tribesmen.

We ride past the gardens and through the shady lanes to our camp, on the outskirts of the modern village. The air is heavy and languid, full of relaxing influence, an air of sloth and luxury, seeming to belong to some strange region below the level of human duty and effort as far as it is below the level of the sea. The fragrance of the orange-blossoms, like a subtle incense of indulgence, floats on the evening breeze. Veiled figures pass us in the lanes, showing lustrous eyes. A sound of Oriental music and laughter and clapping hands comes from one of the houses in an inclosure hedged with acacia-trees. We sit in the door of our tent at sundown and dream of the vanished palm-groves, the gardens of Cleopatra, the palaces of Herod, the soft, ignoble history of that region of fertility and indolence, rich in harvests, poor in manhood.

Then it seems as if some one were saying, "I will lift up mine eyes unto the hills, from whence cometh my help." There they stand, all about us: eastward, the great purple ranges of Gad and Reuben, from which Elijah the Tishbite descended to rebuke and warn Israel; westward, against the saffron sky, the ridges and peaks of Judea, among which Amos and Jeremiah saw their lofty visions; northward, the clear-cut pinnacle of Sartoba, and far away beyond it the dim outlines of the Galilean hills from which Jesus of Nazareth came down to open blind eyes and to shepherd wandering souls. With the fading of the sunset glow a deep blue comes upon all the moun-

tains, a blue which strangely seems to grow paler
as the sky above them darkens, sinking down upon
them through infinite gradations of azure into something mysterious and indescribable, not a color, not
a shadow, not a light, but a secret hyaline illumination which transforms them into aerial battlements
and ramparts, on whose edge the great stars rest and
flame, the watch-fires of the Eternal.

III

"PASSING OVER JORDAN"

I HAVE often wondered why the Jordan, which
plays such an important part in the history of the
Hebrews, receives so little honour and praise in their
literature. Sentimental travellers and poets of other
races have woven a good deal of florid prose and
verse about the name of this river. There is no doubt
that it is the chief stream of Palestine, the only one, in
fact, that deserves to be called a river. Yet the Bible
has no song of loving pride for the Jordan; no tender and beautiful words to describe it; no record of
the longing of exiled Jews to return to the banks of

their own river and hear again the voice of its waters. At this strange silence I have wondered much, not knowing the reason of it. Now I know.

The Jordan is not a little river to be loved: it is a barrier to be passed over. From its beginning in the marshes of Huleh to its end in the Dead Sea, (excepting only the lovely interval of the Lake of Galilee), this river offers nothing to man but danger and difficulty, perplexity and trouble. Fierce and sullen and intractable, it flows through a long depression, at the bottom of which it has dug for itself a still deeper crooked ditch, along the Eastern border of Galilee and Samaria and Judea, as if it wished to cut them off completely. There are no pleasant places along its course, no breezy forelands where a man might build a house with a fair outlook over flowing water, no rich and tranquil coves where the cattle would love to graze, or stand knee-deep in the quiet stream. There is no sense of leisure, of refreshment, of kind companionship and friendly music about the Jordan. It is in a hurry and a secret rage. Yet there is something powerful, self-reliant, inevitable about it. In thousands of years it has changed less than any river in the world. It is a flowing, everlasting symbol of division, of separation: a river of solemn meetings and partings like that of Elijah and Elisha, of Jesus and John the Baptist: a type of the narrow stream of death. It seems to say to man, "Cross me if you will, if you can; and then go your way."

The road that leads us from Jericho toward the river is pleasant enough, at first, for the early sunlight is gentle and caressing, and there is a cool breeze moving across the plain. It is hard to believe that we are eight hundred feet below the sea this morning, and still travelling downward. The lush fields of barley, watered by many channels from the brook Kelt, are waving and glistening around us. Quails are running along the edge of the road, appearing and disappearing among the thick grainstalks. The bulbuls warble from the thorn-bushes, and a crested hoopoo croons in a jujube-tree. Larks are on the wing, scattering music.

We are on the upper edge of that great belt of sunken land between the mountains of Gilead and the mountains of Ephraim and Judah, which reaches from the Lake of Galilee to the Dead Sea, and which the Arabs call *El-Ghôr*, the "Rift." It is a huge trench, from three to fourteen miles wide, sinking from six hundred feet below the level of the Mediterranean, at the northern end, to thirteen hundred feet below, at the southern end. The surface is fairly level, sloping gently from each side toward the middle, and the soil is of an inexhaustible fertility, yielding abundant crops wherever it is patiently irrigated from the streams which flow out of the mountains east and west, but elsewhere lying baked and arid under the heavy, close, feverous air. No strong race has ever inhabited this trench as a home; no great cities have ever grown here, and its civilization, such as it had, was a hot-bed product, soon ripe and quickly rotten.

We have passed beyond the region of greenness already; the little water-brooks have ceased to gleam through the grain: the wild grasses and weeds have a parched and yellow look: the freshness of the early morning has vanished, and we are descending through a desolate land of sour and leprous hills of clay and marl, eroded by the floods into fantastic shapes, furrowed, and scarred and scabbed with mineral refuse. The gullies are steep and narrow: the heat settles on them like a curse.

Through this battered and crippled region, the centre of the Jordan Valley, runs the Jordan Bed, twisting like a big green serpent. A dense half-tropical jungle, haunted by wild beasts and poisonous reptiles and insects, conceals, almost at every point, the down-rushing, swirling, yellow flood.

It has torn and desolated its own shores with sudden spates. The feet of the pilgrims who bathe in it sink into the mud as they wade out waist-deep, and if they venture beyond the shelter of the bank the whirling eddies threaten to sweep them away. The fords are treacherous, with shifting bottom and changing currents. The poets and prophets of the Old Testament give us a true idea of this uninhabitable and unlovable river-bed when they speak of "the pride of Jordan," "the swellings of Jordan," where the lion hides among the reeds in his secret lair, a "refuge of lies," which the "overflowing scourge" shall sweep away.

No, it was not because the Jordan was beautiful

that John the Baptist chose it as the scene of his preaching and ministry, but because it was wild and rude, an emblem of violent and sudden change, of irrevocable parting, of death itself, and because in its one gift of copious and unfailing water, he found the necessary element for his deep baptism of repentance, in which the sinful past of the crowd who followed him was to be symbolically immersed and buried and washed away.

At the place where we reach the water there is an open bit of ground; a miserable hovel gives shelter to two or three Turkish soldiers; an ungainly latticed bridge, stilted on piles of wood, straddles the river with a single span. The toll is three piastres, (about twelve cents,) for a man and horse.

The only place from which I can take a photograph of the river is the bridge itself, so I thrust the camera through one of the diamond-shaped openings on the lattice-work and try to make a truthful record of the lower Jordan at its best. Imagine the dull green of the tangled thickets, the ragged clumps of reeds and water-grasses, the sombre and silent flow of the fulvous water sliding and curling down

146

out of the jungle, and the implacable fervour of the pallid, searching sunlight heightening every touch of ugliness and desolation, and you will understand why the Hebrew poets sang no praise of the Jordan, and why Naaman the Syrian thought scorn of it when he remembered the lovely and fruitful rivers of Damascus.

A PSALM OF RIVERS

The rivers of God are full of water:
They are wonderful in the renewal of their strength:
He poureth them out from a hidden fountain.

They are born among the hills in the high places:
Their cradle is in the bosom of the rocks:
The mountain is their mother and the forest is their
     father.

They are nourished among the long grasses:
They receive the tribute of a thousand springs:
The rain and the snow are a heritage for them.

They are glad to be gone from their birthplace:
With a joyful noise they hasten away:
They are going forever and never departed.

The courses of the rivers are all appointed:
They roar loudly but they follow the road:
The finger of God hath marked their pathway.

The rivers of Damascus rejoice among their gardens:
The great river of Egypt is proud of his ships:
The Jordan is lost in the Lake of Bitterness.

Surely the Lord guideth them every one in his wisdom:
In the end he gathereth all their drops on high:
He sendeth them forth again in the clouds of mercy.

O my God, my life rvnneth away like a river:
Guide me, I beseech thee, in a pathway of good:
Let me flow in blessing to my rest in thee.

VIII

A JOURNEY TO JERASH

THROUGH THE LAND OF GILEAD

I NEVER heard of Jerash until my friend the Archæologist told me about it, one night when we were sitting beside my study fire at Avalon. "It is the site of the old city of Gerasa," said he. "The most satisfactory ruins that I have ever seen."

There was something suggestive and potent in that phrase, "satisfactory ruins." For what is it that weaves the charm of ruins? What do we ask of them to make their magic complete and satisfying? There must be an element of picturesqueness, certainly, to take the eye with pleasure in the contrast between the frailty of man's works and the imperishable loveliness of nature. There must also be an element of age; for new ruins are painful, disquieting, intolerable; they speak of violence and disorder; it is not until the bloom of antiquity gathers upon them that the relics of vast and splendid edifices attract us and subdue us with a spell, breathing tranquillity and noble thoughts. There must also be an element of magnificence in decay, of symmetry broken but not destroyed, a touch of delicate art and workmanship, to quicken the imagination and evoke the ghost of beauty haunting her ancient habitations. And beyond these things I think there must be two more qualities in a ruin that satisfies us: a clear connection with the greatness and glory of the past, with some fine human achievement, with some heroism of men dead and gone; and last of all, a spirit of mystery, the secret of some unexplained catastrophe, the lost link of a story never to be fully told.

This, or something like it, was what the Archæologist's phrase seemed to promise me as we watched the glowing embers on the hearth of Avalon. And it is this promise that has drawn me, with my three friends, on this April day into the Land of Gilead, riding to Jerash.

The grotesque and rickety bridge by which we have crossed the Jordan soon disappears behind us, as we trot along the winding bridle-path through the river-jungle, in the stifling heat. Coming out on the open plain, which rises gently toward the east, we startle great flocks of storks into the air, and they swing away in languid circles, dappling the blaze of morning with their black-tipped wings. Grotesque, ungainly, gothic birds, they do not seem to belong to the Orient, but rather to have drifted hither out of some quaint, familiar fairy tale of the North; and indeed they are only transient visitors here, and will soon be on their way to build their nests on the roofs of German villages and clapper their long, yellow bills over the joy of houses full of little children.

The rains of spring have spread a thin bloom of green over the plain. Tender herbs and light grasses partly veil the gray and stony ground. There is a month of scattered feeding for the flocks and herds. Away to the south, where the foot-hills begin to roll up suddenly from the Jordan, we can see a black line of Bedouin tents quivering through the heat.

Now the trail divides, and we take the northern fork, turning soon into the open mouth of the Wâdi Shaîb, a broad, grassy valley between high and tree-less hills. The watercourse that winds down the middle of it is dry: nothing but a tumbled bed of gray rocks,—the bare bones of a little river. But as we ascend slowly the flowers increase; wild hollyhocks, and morning-glories, and clumps of blue anchusa, and scarlet adonis, and tall wands of white asphodel.

The morning grows hotter and hotter as we plod along. Presently we come up with three mounted Arabs, riding leisurely. Salutations are exchanged with gravity. Then the Arabs whisper something to each other and spur away at a great pace ahead of us—laughing. Why did they laugh?

Ah, now we know. For here is a lofty cliff on one side of the valley, hanging over just far enough to make a strip of cool shade at its base, with ferns and deep grass and a glimmer of dripping water. And here our wise Arabs are sitting at their ease to eat their mid-day meal under "the shadow of a great rock in a weary land."

Vainly we search the valley for another rock like that. It is the only one; and the Arabs laughed because they knew it. We must content ourselves with this little hill where a few hawthorn bushes offer us tiny islets of shade, beset with thorns, and separated by straits of intolerable glare. Here we eat a little, but without comfort; and sleep a little, but without refreshment; and talk a little, but restlessly. As soon as we dare, we get into the saddle again and toil up through the valley, now narrowing into a rugged gorge, crammed with ardent heat. The sprinkling of trees and bushes, the multitude of flowers, assure us that there must be moisture underground, along the bed of the stream; but above ground there is not a drop, and not a breath of wind to break the dead calm of the smothering air. Why did we come into this heat-trap?

But presently the ravine leads us, by steep stairs of rock, up to a high, green table-land. A heavenly breeze from the west is blowing here. The fields are full of flowers—red anemones, white and yellow daisies, pink flax, little blue bell-flowers—a hundred kinds. One knoll is covered with cyclamens; another with splendid purple iris, immense blossoms, so dark that they look almost black against the grass; but hold them up to the sun and you will see the imperial colour. We have never found such wild flowers, not even on the Plain of Sharon; the hills around Jerusalem were but sparsely adorned in comparison with these highlands of bloom.

And here are oak-trees, broad-limbed and friendly, clothed in glistening green. Let us rest for a while in this cool shade and forget the misery of the blazing noon. Below us lies the gray Jordan valley and the steel-blue mirror of the Dead Sea; and across that gulf we see the furrowed mountains of Judea and Samaria, and far to the north the peaks of Galilee. Around us is the Land of Gilead, a rolling hill-country, with long ridges and broad summits, a rounded land, a verdurous land, a land of rich pasturage. There are deep valleys that cut into it and divide it up. But the main bulk of it is lifted high in the air, and spread out nobly to the visitations of the wind. And see—far away there, to the south, across the Wâdi Nimrîn, a mountainside covered with wild trees, a real woodland, almost a forest!

Now we must travel on, for it is still a long way to our night-quarters at Es Salt. We pass several Bedouin camps, the only kind of villages in this part of the world. The tents of goat's-hair are swarming with life. A score of ragged Arab boys are playing hockey on the green with an old donkey's hoof for a ball. They yell with refreshing vigour, just like universal human boys.

The trail grows steeper and more rocky, ascending apparently impossible places, and winding perilously along the cliffs above little vineyards and cultivated fields where men are ploughing. Travel and traffic increase along this rude path, which is the only highway: evidently we are coming near to some place of importance.

But where is Es Salt? For nine hours we have been in the saddle, riding steadily toward that mysterious metropolis of the Belka, the only living city in the Land of Gilead; and yet there is no trace of it in sight. Have we missed the trail? The mule-train with our tents and baggage passed us in the valley while we were sweltering under the hawthorns. It seems as if it must have vanished into the pastoral wilderness and left us travelling an endless road to nowhere.

At last we top a rugged ridge and look down upon the solution of the mystery. Es Salt is a city that can be hid; for it is not set upon a hill, but tucked away in a valley that curves around three sides of a rocky eminence, and is sheltered from the view by higher ranges.

Who can tell how this city came here, hidden in this hollow place almost three thousand feet above the sea? Who was its founder? What was its ancient name? It is a place without traditions, without antiquities, without a shrine of any kind; just a living town, thriving and prospering in its own dirty and dishevelled way, in the midst of a country of nomads, growing in the last twenty years from six thousand to fifteen thousand inhabitants, driving a busy trade with the surrounding country, exporting famous raisins and dye-stuff made from sumach, the seat of the Turkish Government of the Belka, with a garrison and a telegraph office—decidedly a thriving town of to-day; yet without a road by which a carriage can approach it; and old, unmistakably old!

The castle that crowns the eminence in the centre is a ruin of unknown date. The copious spring that gushes from the castle-hill must have invited men for many centuries to build their habitations around it. The gray houses seem to have slipped and settled down into the curving valley, and to have crowded one another up the opposite slopes, as if hundreds of generations had found here a hiding-place and a city of refuge.

We ride through a Mohammedan graveyard— unfenced, broken, neglected—and down a steep, rain-gulleyed hillside, into the filthy, narrow street. The people all have an Arab look, a touch of the wildness of the desert in their eyes and their free bearing. There are many fine figures and handsome faces, some with auburn hair and a reddish hue showing through the bronze of their cheeks. They stare at us with undisguised curiosity and wonder, as if we came from a strange world. The swarthy merchants in the doors of their little shops, the half-veiled women in the lanes, the groups of idlers at the corners of the streets, watch us with a gaze which seems almost defiant. Evidently tourists are a rarity here—perhaps an intrusion to be resented.

We inquire whether our baggage-train has been seen, where our camp is pitched. No one knows, no one cares; until at last a ragged, smiling urchin, one of those blessed, ubiquitous boys who always know everything that happens in a town, offers to guide us. He trots ahead, full of importance, dodging through the narrow alleys, making the complete circuit of the castle-hill and leading us to the upper end of the eastern valley. Here, among a few olive-trees beside the road, our white tents are standing, so close to an encampment of wandering gypsies that the tent-ropes cross.

Directly opposite rises a quarter of the town, tier upon tier of flat-roofed houses, every roof-top covered with people. A wild-looking crowd of visitors have gathered in the road. Two soldiers, with the appearance of partially reformed brigands, are acting as our guard, and keeping the inquisitive spectators at a respectful distance. Our mules and donkeys and horses are munching their supper in a row, tethered to a long rope in front of the tents. Shukari, the cook, in his white cap and apron, is gravely intent upon the operation of his little charcoal range. Youssouf, the major-domo, is setting the table with flowers and lighted candles in the dining-tent. After a while he comes to the door of our sleeping-tents to inform us, with due ceremony, that dinner is served; and we sit down to our repast in the midst of the swarming Edomites and the wandering Zingari as peacefully and properly as if we were dining at the Savoy.

The night darkens around us. Lights twinkle, one above another, up the steep hillside of houses; above them are the tranquil stars, the lit windows of unknown habitations; and on the hill-top one great planet burns in liquid flame.

The crowd melts away, chattering down the road; it forms again, from another quarter, and again dissolves. Meaningless shouts and cries and songs resound from the hidden city. In the gypsy camp beside us insomnia reigns. A little forge is clinking and clanking. Donkeys raise their antiphonal lament. Dogs salute the stars in chorus. First a leader, far away, lifts a wailing, howling, shrieking note; then the mysterious unrest that torments the bosom of Oriental dogdom breaks loose in a hundred, a thousand answering voices, swelling into a yapping, growling, barking, yelling discord. A sudden silence cuts the tumult short, until once more the unknown misery, (or is it the secret joy), of the canine heart bursts out in long-drawn dissonance.

From the road and from the tents of the gypsies various human voices are sounding close around us all the night. Through our confused dreams and broken sleep we strangely seem to catch fragments of familiar speech, phrases of English or French or German. Then, waking and listening, we hear men muttering and disputing, women complaining or soothing their babies, children quarrelling or calling to each other, in Arabic, or Romany—not a word that we can understand—voices that tell us only that we are in a strange land, and very far away from home, camping in the heart of a wild city.

II

OVER THE BROOK JABBOK

AFTER such a night the morning is welcome, as it breaks over the eastern hill behind us, with rosy light creeping slowly down the opposite slope of houses. Before the sunbeams have fairly reached the bottom of the valley we are in the saddle, ready to leave Es Salt without further exploration.

There is a general monotony about this riding through Palestine which yet leaves room for a particular variety of the most entrancing kind. Every day is like every other in its main outline, but the details are infinitely uncertain—always there is something new, some touch of a distinct and memorable charm.

To-day it is the sense of being in the country of the nomads, the tent-dwellers, the masters of innumerable flocks and herds, whose wealth goes wandering from pasture to pasture, bleating and lowing and browsing and multiplying over the open moorland beneath the blue sky. This is the prevailing impression of this day: and the symbol of it is the thin, quavering music of the pastoral pipe, following us wherever we go, drifting tremulously and plaintively down from some rock on the hillside, or floating up softly from some hidden valley, where a brown shepherd or goatherd is minding his flock with music.

What quaint and rustic melodies are these! Wild and unfamiliar to our ears; yet doubtless the same wandering airs that were played by the sons and servants of Jacob when he returned from his twenty years of profitable exile in Haran with his rich wages of sheep and goats and cattle and wives and maid-servants, the fruit of his hard labour and shrewd bargaining with his father-in-law Laban, and passed cautiously through Gilead on his way to the Promised Land.

On the highland to the east of Es Salt we see a fine herd of horses, brood-mares and foals. A little farther on, we come to a muddy pond or tank at which a drove of asses are drinking. A steep and winding path, full of loose stones, leads us down into a grassy, oval plain, a great cup of green, eight or ten miles long and five or six miles wide, rimmed with bare hills from five to eight hundred feet high. This, we conjecture, is the fertile basin of El Buchaia, or Bekaa.

Bedouin farmers are ploughing the rich, reddish soil. Their black tent-villages are tucked away against the feet of the surrounding hills. The broad plain itself is without sign of human dwelling, except that near each focus of the ellipse there is a pile of shattered ruins with a crumbling, solitary tower, where a shepherd sits piping to his lop-eared flock.

In one place we pass through a breeding-herd of camels, browsing on the short grass. The old ones are in the process of the spring moulting; their thick, matted hair is peeling off in large flakes, like fragments of a ragged, moth-eaten coat. The young ones are covered with pearl-gray wool, soft and almost downy, like gigantic goslings with four legs. (What is the word for a young camel, I wonder; is is camelet or camelot?) But young and old have a family resemblance of ugliness.

The camel is the most ungainly and stupid of God's useful beasts—an awkward necessity—the humpbacked ship of the desert. The Arabs have a story which runs thus: "What did Allah say when He had finished making the camel? He couldn't say anything; He just looked at the camel, and laughed, and laughed!"

But in spite of his ridiculous appearance the camel seems satisfied with himself; in fact there is an expression of supreme contempt in his face when he droops his pendulous lower lip and wrinkles his nose, which has led the Arabs to tell another story about him: "Why does the camel despise his master? Because man knows only the ninety-nine common names of Allah; but the hundredth name, the wonderful name, the beautiful name, is a secret revealed to the camel alone. Therefore he scorns the whole race of men."

The cattle that feed around the edges of this peaceful plain are small and nimble, as if they were used to long, rough journeys. The prevailing colour is black, or rusty brown. They are evidently of a degenerate and played-out stock. Even the heifers are used for ploughing, and they look but little larger than the donkeys which are often yoked beside them. They come around the grassy knoll when our luncheon-tent is pitched, and stare at us very much as the people stared in Es Salt.

In the afternoon we pass over the rim of the broad vale and descend a narrower ravine, where oaks and terebinths, laurels and balsams, pistachios and almonds are growing. The grass springs thick and lush, tall weeds and trailing vines appear, a murmur of flowing water is heard under the tangled herbage at the bottom of the wâdi. Presently we are following a bright little brook, crossing and recrossing it as it leads us toward our camp-ground.

There are the tents, standing in a line on the flowery bank of the brook, across the water from the trail. A few steps lower down there is a well-built stone basin with a copious spring gushing into it from the hillside under an arched roof. Here the people of the village, (which is somewhere near us on the mountain, but out of sight), come to fill their pitchers and water-skins, and to let their cattle and donkeys drink. All through the late afternoon they are coming and going, plashing through the shallow ford below us, enjoying the cool, clear water, disappearing along the foot-paths that lead among the hills.

These are very different cattle from the herds we saw among the Bedouins a couple of hours ago; fine large creatures, well bred and well fed, some cream-coloured, some red, some belted with white. And these men who follow them, on foot or on horseback, truculent looking fellows with blue eyes and light hair and broad faces, clad in long, close-fitting tunics, with belts around their waists and small black caps of fur, some of them with high boots—who are they?

They are some of the Circassian immigrants who were driven out of Russia by the Czar after the Russo-Turkish War of 1877, and deported again after the Bulgarian atrocities, and whom the Turkish Government has colonized through eastern Palestine on land given by the Sultan. Nobody really knows to whom the land belongs, I suppose; but the Bedouins have had the habit, for many centuries, of claiming and using it as they pleased for their roaming flocks and herds. Now these northern invaders are taking and holding the most fertile places, the best springs, the fields that are well watered through the year.

Therefore the Arab hates the Circassian, though

he be of the same religion, far more than he hates the Christian, almost as much as he hates the Turk. But the Circassian can take care of himself; he is a fierce and hardy fighter; and in his rude way he understands how to make farming and stock-raising pay.

Indeed, this Land of Gilead is a region in which twenty times the present population, if they were industrious and intelligent and had good government, might prosper. No wonder that the tribe of Gad and Reuben and the half-tribe of Manasseh, on the way to Canaan, "when they saw the land of Jazer and the land of Gilead, that, behold, the place was a place for cattle," (Numbers xxxii) fell in love with it, and besought Moses that they might have their inheritance there, and not westward of the Jordan. No wonder that they recrossed the river after they had helped Joshua to conquer the Canaanites, and settled in this high country, so much fairer and more fertile than Judea, or even than Samaria.

It was here, in 1880, that Laurence Oliphant, the gifted English traveller and mystic, proposed to establish his fine scheme for the beginning of the restoration of the Jews to Palestine. A territory extending from the brook of Jabbok on the north to the brook of Arnon on the south, from the Jordan Valley on the west to the Arabian desert on the east; railways running up from the sea at Haifa, and down from Damascus, and southward to the Gulf of Akabah, and across to Ismailia on the Suez Canal; a government of local autonomy guaranteed and protected by the Sublime Porte; sufficient capital supplied by the Jewish bankers of London and Paris and Berlin and Vienna; and the outcasts of Israel gathered from all the countries where they are oppressed, to dwell together in peace and plenty, tending sheep and cattle, raising fruit and grain, pressing out wine and oil, and supplying the world with the balm of Gilead—such was Oliphant's beautiful dream.

But it did not come true; because Russia did not like it, because Turkey was afraid of it, because the rest of Europe did not care for it,—and perhaps because the Jews themselves were not generally enthusiastic over it. Perhaps the majority of them would rather stay where they are. Perhaps

they do not yearn passionately for Palestine and
the simple life.

But it is not of these things that we are thinking,
I must confess, as the ruddy sun slowly drops toward
the heights of Pennel, and we stroll out in the evening glow, along the edge of the wild ravine into
which our little stream plunges, and look down into
the deep, grand valley of the Brook Jabbok.

Yonder, on the other side of the great gulf of
heliotrope shadow, stretches the long bulk of the
Jebel Ajlûn, shaggy with oak-trees. It was somewhere on the slopes of that wooded mountain that
one of the most tragic battles of the world was fought.
For there the army of Absalom went out to meet the
army of his father David. "And the battle was
spread over the face of all the country, and the forest
devoured more people that day than the sword devoured." It was there that the young man Absalom
rode furiously upon his mule, "and the mule went
under the thick boughs of a great oak, and his head
caught hold of the oak, and he was taken up between
heaven and earth." And a man came and told Joab,
the captain of David's host, "Behold I saw Absalom

hanging in the midst of an oak." Then Joab made haste; "and he took three darts in his hand, and thrust them through the heart of Absalom while he was yet alive in the midst of the oak." And when the news came to David, sitting in the gate of the city of Mahanaim, he went up into the chamber over the gate and wept bitterly, crying, "Would I had died for thee, O Absalom, my son!" (II Samuel xviii.)

To remember a story like that is to feel the pathos with which man has touched the face of nature. But there is another story, more mystical, more beautiful, which belongs to the scene upon which we are looking. Down in the purple valley, where the smooth meadows spread so fair, and the little river curves and gleams through the thickets of oleander, somewhere along that flashing stream is the place where Jacob sent his wives and his children, his servants and his cattle, across the water in the darkness, and there remained all night long alone, for "there wrestled a man with him until the breaking of the day."

Who was this "man" with whom the patriarch

contended at midnight, and to whom he cried, "I will not let thee go except thou bless me"? On the morrow Jacob was to meet his fierce and powerful brother Esau, whom he had wronged and outwitted, from whom he had stolen the birthright blessing twenty years before. Was it the prospect of this dreaded meeting that brought upon Jacob the night of lonely struggle by the Brook Jabbok? Was it the promise of reconciliation with his brother that made him say at dawn, "I have seen God face to face, and my life is saved"? Was it the unexpected friendliness and gentleness of that brother in the encounter of the morning that inspired Jacob's cry, "I have seen *thy face as one seeth the face of God*, and thou wast pleased with me"?

Yes, that *is* what the old story means, in its Oriental imagery. The midnight wrestling is the pressure of human enmity and strife. The morning peace is the assurance of human forgiveness and love. The face of God seen in the face of human kindness—that is the sunrise vision of the Brook Jabbok.

Such are the thoughts with which we fall asleep

in our tents beside the murmuring brook of **Er
Rumman**. Early the next morning we go down,
and down, and down, by ledge and terrace and
grassy slope, into the Vale of Jabbok. It is sixty
miles long, beginning on the edge of the mountain
of Moab, and curving eastward, northward, westward, south-westward, between Gilead and Ajlûn,
until it opens into the Jordan Valley.

Here is the famous little river, a swift, singing
current of gray-blue water—Nahr ez-Zerka "blue
river," the Arabs call it—dashing and swirling
merrily between the thickets of willows and tama-
racks and oleanders that border it. The ford is
rather deep, for the spring flood is on; but our
horses splash through gaily, scattering the water
around them in showers which glitter in the sunshine.

Is this the brook beside which a man once met
God? Yes—and by many another brook too.

III

THE RUINS OF GERASA

WE are coming now into the region of the Decapolis, the Greek cities which sprang up along the eastern border of Palestine after the conquests of Alexander the Great.

They were trading cities, undoubtedly, situated on the great roads which led from the east across the desert to the Jordan Valley, and so, converging upon the Plain of Esdraelon, to the Mediterranean Sea and to Greece and Italy. Their wealth tempted the Jewish princes of the Hasmonean line to conquer and plunder them; but the Roman general Pompey restored their civic liberties, B. C. 65, and caused them to be rebuilt and strengthened. By the beginning of the Christian era, they were once more rich and flourishing, and a league was formed of ten municipalities, with certain rights of communal and local government, under the protection and suzerainty of the Roman Empire.

The ten cities which originally composed this confederacy for mutual defence and the development of their trade, were Scythopolis, Hippos, Damascus, Gadara, Raphana, Kanatha, Pella, Dion, Philadelphia and Gerasa. Their money was stamped with the image of Cæsar. Their soldiers followed the Imperial eagles. Their traditions, their arts, their literature were Greek. But their strength and their new prosperity were Roman.

Here in this narrow wâdi through which we are climbing up from the Vale of Jabbok we find the traces of the presence of the Romans in the fragments of a paved military road and an aqueduct. Presently we surmount a rocky hill and look down into the broad, shallow basin of Jerash. Gently sloping, rock-strewn hills surround it; through the centre flows a stream, with banks bordered by trees; a water-fall is flashing opposite to us; on a cluster of rounded knolls about the middle of the valley, on the west bank of the stream, are spread the vast, incredible, complete ruins of the ancient city of Gerasa.

They rise like a dream in the desolation of the wilderness, columns and arches and vaults and amphitheatres and temples, suddenly appearing in the bare and lonely landscape as if by enchantment.

How came these monuments of splendour and permanence into this country of simplicity and transience, this land of shifting shepherds and drovers, this empire of the black tent, this immemorial region that has slept away the centuries under the spell of the pastoral pipe? What magical music of another kind, strong, stately and sonorous, music of brazen trumpets and shawms, of silver harps and cymbals, evoked this proud and potent city on the border of the desert, and maintained for centuries, amid the sweeping, turbulent floods of untamable tribes of rebels and robbers, this lofty landmark of

> "the glory that was Greece
> And the grandeur that was Rome"?

What sudden storm of discord and disaster shook it all down again, loosened the sinews of majesty and power, stripped away the garments of beauty and luxury, dissolved the lovely body of living joy, and left this skeleton of dead splendour diffused upon the solitary ground?

Who can solve these mysteries? It is all unaccountable, unbelievable,—the ghost of the dream of a dream,—yet here it is, surrounded by the green hills, flooded with the frank light of noon, neighboured by a dirty, noisy little village of Arabs and Circassians on the east bank of the stream, and with real goats and lean, black cattle grazing between the carved columns and under the broken architraves of Gerasa the Golden.

Let us go up into the wrecked city.

This triumphal arch, with its three gates and its lofty Corinthian columns, stands outside of the city walls: a structure which has no other use or meaning than the expression of Imperial pride: thus the Roman conquerors adorn and approach their vassal-town.

Behind the arch a broad, paved road leads to the southern gate, perhaps a thousand feet away. Beside the road, between the arch and the gate, lie two buildings of curious interest. The first is a great pool of stone, seven hundred feet long by three hundred feet wide. This is the Naumachia, which is filled with water by conduits from the neighbouring stream, in order that the Greeks may hold their mimic naval combats and regattas here in the desert, for they are always at heart a seafaring people. Beyond the pool there is a Circus, with four rows of stone seats and an oval arena, for wild-beast shows and gladiatorial combats.

The city walls have almost entirely disappeared and the South Gate is in ruins. Entering and turning to the left, we ascend a little hill and find the Temple (perhaps dedicated to Artemis), and close beside it the great South Theatre. There is hardly a break in the semicircular stone benches, thirty-two rows of seats rising tier above tier, divided into an upper and a lower section by a broader row of "boxes" or stalls, richly carved, and reserved, no doubt, for magnates of the city and persons of importance. The stage, over a hundred feet wide, is backed by a straight wall adorned with Corinthian columns and decorated niches. The theatre faces due north; and the spectator sitting here, if the play wearies him, can lift his eyes and look off beyond the proscenium over the length and breadth of Gerasa.

181

A JOURNEY TO JERASH

"But he looked upon the city, every side,
                    Far and wide,
All the mountains topped with temples, all the glades
                    Colonnades,
All the causeys, bridges, acqueducts,—and then,
                    All the men!"

In the hollow northward from this theatre is the Forum, or the Market-place, or the Hippodrome— I cannot tell what it is, but a splendid oval of Ionic pillars incloses an open space of more than three hundred feet in length and two hundred and fifty feet in width, where the Gerasenes may barter or bicker or bet, as they will.

From the Forum to the North Gate runs the main street, more than half a mile long, lined with a double row of columns, from twenty to thirty feet high, with smooth shafts and acanthus capitals. At the intersection of the cross-streets there are tetra-pylons, with domes, and pedestals for statues. The pavement of the roadway is worn into ruts by the chariot wheels. Under the arcades behind the columns run the sidewalks for foot-passengers. Turn to the right from the main street and you come to the Public Baths, an immense building like a palace, supplied with hot and cold water, adorned with marble and mosaic. On the left lies the Tribuna, with its richly decorated façade and its fountain of flowing water. A few yards farther north is the Propylæum of the Great Temple; a superb gateway, decorated with columns and garlands and shell niches, opening to a wide flight of steps by which we ascend to the temple-area, a terrace nearly twice the size of Madison Square Garden, surrounded by two hundred and sixty columns, and standing clear above the level of the encircling city.

The Temple of the Sun rises at the western end of this terrace, facing the dawn. The huge columns of the portico, forty-five feet high and five feet in diameter, with rich Corinthian capitals, are of rosy-yellow limestone, which seems to be saturated with the sunshine of a thousand years. Behind them are the walls of the Cella, or inner shrine, with its vaulted apse for the image of the god, and its secret stairs and passages in the rear wall for the coming and going of the priests, and the ascent to the roof for the first salutation of the sunrise over the eastern hills.

Spreading our cloth between two pillars of the portico we celebrate the feast of noontide, and looking out over the wrecked magnificence of the city we try to reconstruct the past.

It was in the days of Antoninus Pius and Marcus Aurelius, in the latter part of the second century after Christ, that these temples and palaces and theatres were rising. Those were the palmy days of Græco-Roman civilisation in Syria; then the shops along the Colonnade were filled with rich goods, the Forum listened to the voice of world-famous orators and teachers, and proud lords and ladies assembled in the Naumachia to watch the sham battles of the miniature galleys. A little later the new religion of Christianity found a foothold here, (see, these are the ruined outlines of a Christian church below us to the south, and the foundation of a great Basilica), and by the fifth century the pagan worship was dying out, and the Bishop of Gerasa had a seat in the Council of Chalcedon. It was no longer with the comparative merits of Stoicism and Epicureanism and Neo-Platonism, or with the rival literary fame of their own Ariston and Kerykos as against Meleager and Me-

Ruins of Jerash, Looking West.
Propylaeum and Temple terrace.

nippus and Theodorus of Gadara, that the Gerasenes concerned themselves. They were busy now with the controversies about Homoiousia and Homoöusia, with the rivalry of the Eutychians and the Nestorians, with the conflicting, not to say combative, claims of such saints as Dioscurus of Alexandria and Theodoret of Cyrus. But trade continued brisk, and the city was as rich and as proud as ever. In the seventh century an Arabian chronicler named it among the great towns of Palestine, and a poet praised its fertile territory and its copious spring.

Then what happened? Earthquake, pestilence, conflagration, pillage, devastation—who knows? A Mohammedan writer of the thirteenth century merely mentions it as "a great city of ruins"; and so it lay, deserted and forgotten, until a German traveller visited it in 1806; and so it lies to-day, with all its dwellings and its walls shattered and dissolved beside its flowing stream in the centre of its green valley, and only the relics of its temples, its theatres, its colonnades, and its triumphal arch remaining to tell us how brave and rich and gay it was in the days of old.

Do you believe it? Does it seem at all real or possible to you? Look up at this tall pillar above us. See how the wild marjoram has thrust its roots between the joints and hangs like "the hyssop that springeth out of the wall." See how the weather has worn deep holes and crevices in the topmost drum, and how the sparrows have made their nests there. Lean your back against the pillar; feel it vibrate like "a reed shaken with the wind"; watch that huge capital of acanthus leaves swaying slowly to and fro and trembling upon its stalk "as a flower of the field."

All the afternoon and all the next morning we wander through the ruins, taking photographs, deciphering inscriptions, discovering new points of view to survey the city. We sit on the arch of the old Roman bridge which spans the stream, and look down into the valley filled with gardens and orchards; tall poplars shiver in the breeze; peaches, plums, and cherries are in bloom; almonds clad in pale-green foliage; figs putting forth their verdant shoots; pomegranates covered with ruddy young leaves. We go up to see the beautiful spring which bursts from the hillside above the town and supplies it with water. Then we go back again to roam aimlessly and dreamily, like folk bewitched, among the tumbled heaps of hewn stones, the broken capitals, and the tall, rosy columns, soaked with sunbeams.

The Arabs of Jerash have a bad reputation as robbers and extortionists; and in truth they are rather a dangerous-looking lot of fellows, with bold, handsome brown faces and inscrutable dark eyes. But although we have paid no tribute to them, they do not molest us. They seem to regard us with a contemptuous pity, as harmless idiots who loaf among the fallen stones and do not even attempt to make excavations.

Our camp is in the inclosure of the North Theatre, a smaller building than that which stands beside the South Gate, but large enough to hold an audience of two or three thousand. The semicircle of seats is still unbroken; the arrangements of the stage, the stairways, the entries of the building can all be easily traced.

There were gay times in the city when these two

theatres were filled with people. What comedies of Plautus or Terence or Aristophanes or Menander; what tragedies of Seneca, or of the seven dramatists of Alexandria who were called the "Pleias," were presented here?

Look up along those lofty tiers of seats in the pale, clear starlight. Can you see no shadowy figures sitting there, hear no light whisper of ghostly laughter, no thin ripple of clapping hands? What flash of wit amuses them, what nobly tragic word or action stirs them to applause? What problem of their own life, what reflection of their own heart, does the stage reveal to them? We shall never know. The play at Gerasa is ended.

A PSALM AMONG THE RUINS

*The lizard rested on the rock while I sat among the
    ruins;*
*And the pride of man was like a vision of the
    night.*

*Lo, the lords of the city have disappeared into dark-
    ness;*
*The ancient wilderness hath swallowed up all their
    work.*

*There is nothing left of the city but a heap of frag-
    ments;*
*The bones of a carcass that a wild beast hath de-
    voured.*

*Behold the desert waiteth hungrily for man's dwell-
    ings;*
*Surely the tide of desolation returneth upon his
    toil.*

*All that he hath painfully lifted up is shaken down
    in a moment;*
*The memory of his glory is buried beneath the billows
    of sand.*

Then a voice said, Look again upon the ruins;
These broken arches have taught generations to build

Moreover the name of this city shall be remembered;
Here a poor man spoke a word that shall not die.

This is the glory that is stronger than the desert;
For God hath given eternity to the thought of man.

IX

THE MOUNTAINS OF SAMARIA

I

JORDAN FERRY

LOOK down from these tranquil heights of Jebel Osha, above the noiseful, squalid little city of Es Salt, and you see what Moses saw when he climbed Mount Pisgah and looked upon the Promised Land which he was never to enter.

> "Could we but climb where Moses stood,
>   And view the landscape o'er,
> Not Jordan's stream, nor death's cold flood,
>   Should fright us from the shore."

Pisgah was probably a few miles south of the place where we are now standing, but the main features of the view are the same. These broad mountain-shoulders, falling steeply away to the west, clad in the emerald robe of early spring; this immense gulf at our feet, four thousand feet below us, a huge trough of gray and yellow, through which the dark-green ribbon of the Jordan jungle, touched with a few silvery gleams of water, winds to the blue basin of the Dead Sea; those scarred and wrinkled hills rising on the other side, the knotted brow of Quarantana, the sharp cone of Sartoba, the distant peak of Mizpeh, the long line of Judean, Samarian, and Galilean summits, Olivet, and Ebal, and Gerizim, and Gilboa, and Tabor, rolling away to the northward, growing ever fairer with the promise of fertile valleys between them and rich plains beyond them, and fading at last into the azure vagueness of the highlands round the Lake of Galilee.

Why does that country toward which we are looking and travelling seem to us so much more familiar and real, so much more a part of the actual world, than this region of forgotten Greek and Roman .glory, from which we are returning like those who awake from sleep? The ruined splendours of Jerash fade behind us like a dream. Samaria and Galilee, crowded with memories and associations which have been woven into our minds by the wonderful Bible story, draw us to them with the convincing touch of reality. Yet even while we recognise this strange

194

difference between our feelings toward the Holy Land and those toward other parts of the ancient world, we know that it is not altogether true.

Gerasa was as really a part of God's big world as Shechem or Jezreel or Sychar. It stood in His sight, and He must have regarded the human souls that lived there. He must have cared for them, and watched over them, and judged them equitably, dividing the just from the unjust, the children of love from the children of hate, even as He did with men on the other side of the Jordan, even as He does with all men everywhere to-day. If faith in a God who is the Father and Lord of all mankind means any-thing it means this: equal care, equal justice, equal mercy for all the world. Gerasa has been forgotten of men, but God never forgot it.

What, then, is the difference? Just this: in the little land between the Jordan and the sea, things came to pass which have a more enduring signifi-cance than the wars and splendours, the wealth and culture of the Decapolis. Conflicts were fought there in which the eternal issues of good and evil were clearly manifest. Ideas were worked out there which

195

have a permanent value to the spiritual life of man.
Revelations were made there which have become the
guiding stars of succeeding generations. This is
why that country of the Bible seems more real to us:
because its history is more significant, because it is
Divinely inspired with a meaning for our faith and
hope.

Do you agree with this? I do not know. But at
least if you were with us on this glorious morning,
riding down from the heights of Jebel Osha you
would feel the vivid beauty, the subduing grandeur
of the scene. You would rejoice in the life-renewing
air that blows softly around us and invites us to
breathe deep,—in the pure morning faces of the
flowers opening among the rocks,—in the light
waving of silken grasses along the slopes by which
we steeply descend.

There is a young Gileadite running beside us, a
fine fellow about eighteen years old, with his white
robe girded up about his loins, leaving his brown
legs bare. His head-dress is encircled with the black
'agâl of camel's hair like a rustic crown. A long
gun is slung over his back; a wicked-looking curved

knife with a brass sheath sticks in his belt; his silver powder-horn and leather bullet-pouch hang at his waist. He strides along with a free, noble step, or springs lightly from rock to rock like a gazelle.

His story is a short one, and simple,—if true. His younger brother has run away from the family tent among the pastures of Gilead, seeking his fortune in the wide world. And now this elder brother has come out to look for the prodigal, at Nablûs, at Jaffa, at Jerusalem,—Allah knows how far the quest may lead! But he is afraid of robbers if he crosses the Jordan Valley alone. May he keep company with us and make the perilous transit under our august protection? Yes, surely, my brown son of Esau; and we will not inquire too closely whether you are really running after your brother or running away yourself.

There may be a thousand robbers concealed along the river-bed, but we can see none of them. The valley is heat and emptiness. Even the jackal that slinks across the trail in front of us, droops and drags his tail in visible exhaustion. His lolling, red tongue is a signal of distress. In a climate like this one expects nothing from man or beast. Life degenerates, shrivels, stifles; and in the glaring open spaces a sullen madness lurks invisible.

We are coming to the ancient fording-place of the river, called Adamah, where an event once happened which was of great consequence to the Israelites and which has often been misunderstood. They were encamped on the east side, opposite Jericho, nearly thirty miles below this point, waiting for their first opportunity to cross the Jordan. Then, says the record, "the waters which came down from above stopped, and were piled up in a heap, a great way off, at Adam, . . . and the people passed over right against Jericho." (Joshua iii: 14–16.)

Look at these great clay-banks overhanging the river, and you will understand what it was that opened a dry path for Israel into Canaan. One of these huge masses of clay was undermined, and slipped, and fell across the river, heaping up the waters behind a temporary natural dam, and cutting off the supply of the lower stream. It may have taken three or four days for the river to carve its way through or around that obstruction, and meantime any one could march across to Jericho without wetting his feet. I have seen precisely the same thing happen on a salmon river in Canada quite as large as the Jordan.

The river is more open at this place, and there is a curious six-cornered ferry-boat, pulled to and fro with ropes by a half-dozen bare-legged Arabs. If it had been a New England river, the practical Western mind would have built a long boat with a flat board at each side, and rigged a couple of running wheels on a single rope. Then the ferryman would have had nothing to do but let the stern of his craft swing down at an angle with the stream, and the swift current would have pushed him from one side to the other at his will. But these Orientals have been running their ferry in their own way, no doubt, for many centuries; and who are we to break in upon their laborious indolence with new ideas? It is enough that they bring us over safely, with our cattle and our stuff, in several bands, with much tugging at the ropes and shouting and singing.

We look in vain on the shore of the Jordan for a

pleasant place to eat our luncheon. The big trees stand with their feet in the river, and the smaller shrubs are scraggly and spiny. At last we find a little patch of shade on a steep bank above the yellow stream, and here we make ourselves as comfortable as we can, with the thermometer at 110°, and the hungry gnats and mosquitoes swarming around us.

Early in the afternoon we desperately resolve to brave the sun, and ride up from the river-bed into the open plain on the west. Here we catch our first clear view of Mount Hermon, with its mantle of glistening snow, hanging like a cloud on the northern horizon, ninety miles away, beyond the Lake of Galilee and the Waters of Merom; a vision of distance and coolness and grandeur.

The fields, watered by the full streams descending from the Wâdi Fârah, are green with wheat and barley. Along our path are balsam-trees and thorny jujubes, from whose branches we pluck the sweet, insipid fruit as we ride beneath them. Herds of cattle are pasturing on the plain, and long rows of black Bedouin tents are stretched at the foot of the mountains. We cross a dozen murmuring water-courses embowered in the dark, glistening foliage of the oleanders glowing with great soft flames of rosy bloom.

At the Serâi on the hill which watches over this Jiftlîk, or domain of the Sultan, there are some Turkish soldiers saddling their horses for an expedition; perhaps to collect taxes or to chase robbers. The peasants are returning, by the paths among the corn-fields, to their huts. The lines of camp-fires begin to gleam from the transient Bedouin villages. Our white tents are pitched in a flowery meadow, beside a low-voiced stream, and as we fall asleep the night air is trembling with the shrill, innumerable *brek-ek-ek-coäx-coäx* of the frog chorus.

II

MOUNT EPHRAIM AND JACOB'S WELL

SAMARIA is a mountain land, but its characteristic features, as distinguished from Judea, are the easiness of approach through open gateways among the hills, and the fertility of the broad vales and level plains which lie between them. The Kingdom of Israel, in its brief season of prosperity, was richer, more luxurious, and weaker than the Kingdom of Judah. The poet Isaiah touched the keynote of the northern kingdom when he sang of "the crown of pride of the drunkards of Ephraim," and "the fading flower of his glorious beauty which is on the head of the fat valley." (Isaiah xxviii: 1–6.)

We turn aside from the open but roundabout way of the well-tilled Wâdi Fârah and take a shorter, steeper path toward Shechem, through a deep, narrow mountain gorge. The day is hot and hazy, for the Sherkîyeh is blowing from the desert across the Jordan Valley: the breath of Jehovah's displeasure with His people, "a dry wind of the high places of the wilderness toward the daughter of my people, neither to fan nor to cleanse."

At times the walls of rock come so close together that we have to wind through a passage not more than ten feet wide. The air is parched as in an oven. Our horses scramble wearily up the stony gallery and the rough stairways. One of our company faints under the fervent heat, and falls from his horse. But fortunately no bones are broken; a half-hour's rest in the shadow of a great rock revives him and we ride on.

The wonderful flowers are blooming wherever they can find a foothold among the stones. Now and then we cross the mouth of some little lonely side-valley, full of mignonette and cyclamens and tall spires of pink hollyhock. Under the huge, dark sides of Eagle's Crag—bare and rugged as Ben Nevis —we pass into the fruitful plain of Makhna, where the silken grainfields rustle far and wide, and the rich olive-orchards on the hill-slopes offer us a shelter for our midday meal and siesta. Mount Ebal and Mount Gerizim now rise before us in their naked bulk; and, as we mount toward the valley which lies between them, we stay for a while to rest at Jacob's Well.

There is a mystery about this ancient cistern on the side of the mountain. Why was it dug here, a hundred feet deep, although there are springs and streams of living water flowing down the valley, close at hand? Whence came the tradition of the Samaritans that Jacob gave them this well, although the Old Testament says nothing about it? Why did the Samaritan woman, in Jesus' time, come hither to draw water when there was a brook, not fifty yards away, which she must cross to get to the well?

Who can tell? Certainly there must have been some use and reason for such a well, else the men of long ago would never have toiled to make it. Perhaps the people of Sychar had some superstition about its water which made them prefer it. Or perhaps the stream was owned and used for other purposes, while the water of the well was free.

It makes no difference whether a solution of the problem is ever found. Its very existence adds to the touch of truth in the narrative of St. John's Gospel. Certainly this well was here in Jesus' day, close beside the road which He would be most likely to take in going from Jerusalem to Galilee. Here He sat, alone and weary, while the disciples went on to the village to buy food. And here, while He waited and thirsted, He spoke to an unknown, unfriendly, unhappy woman the words which have been a spring of living water to the weary and fevered heart of the world: "God is a spirit, and they that worship Him must worship Him in spirit and in truth."

III

NABLÛS AND SEBASTE

About a mile from Jacob's Well, the city of Nablus lies in the hollow between Mount Gerizim on the south and Mount Ebal on the north. The side of Gerizim is precipitous and jagged; Ebal rises more smoothly, but very steeply, and is covered with plantations of thornless cactus, (*Opuntia cochinillifera*), cultivated for the sake of the cochineal insects which live upon the plant and from which a red dye is made.

The valley is well watered, and is about a quarter of a mile wide. A little east of the city there are two natural bays or amphitheatres opposite to each other in the mountains. Here the tribes of Israel may have been gathered while the priests chanted the curses of the law from Ebal and the blessings from Gerizim. (Joshua viii: 30–35.) The cliffs were sounding-boards and sent the loud voices of blessing and cursing out over the multitude so that all could hear.

It seems as if it were mainly the echo of the cursing of Ebal that greets us as we ride around the fierce little Mohammedan city of Nablûs on Friday afternoon, passing through the open and dilapidated cemeteries where the veiled women are walking and gossiping away their holiday. The looks of the inhabitants are surly and hostile. The children shout mocking ditties at us, reviling the "Nazarenes." We will not ask our dragoman to translate the words that we catch now and then; it is easy to guess that they are not "fit to print."

Our camp is close beside a cemetery, near the eastern gate of the town. The spectators who watch us from a distance while we dine are numerous; and no doubt they are passing unfavourable criticisms on our table manners, and on the Frankish custom of permitting one unveiled lady to travel with three husbands. The population of Nablûs is about twenty-five thousand. It has a Turkish governor, a garrison, several soap factories, and a million dogs which howl all night.

At half-past six the next morning we set out on foot to climb Mount Ebal, which is three thousand feet high. The view from the rocky summit sweeps over all Palestine, from snowy Hermon to the mountains round about Jerusalem, from Carmel to Nebo, from the sapphire expanse of the Mediterranean to the violet valley of the Jordan and the garnet wall of Moab and Gilead beyond.

For us the view is veiled in mystery by the haze of the south wind. The ranges and peaks far away fade into cloudlike shadows. The depths below us seem to sink unfathomably. Nablûs is buried in the gulf. On the summit of Gerizim, a Mohammedan *weli*, shining like a flake of mica, marks the plateau where the Samaritan Temple stood. Hilltop towns, Asîret, Tallûza, Yasîd, emerge like islands from the misty sea. In that great shadowy hollow to the west lie the ruins of the city of Samaria, which Cæsar Augustus renamed Sebaste, in honour of his wife Augusta. If she could see the village of Sebastiyeh now she would not be proud of her namesake town. It is there that we are going to make our midday camp.

King Omri acted as a wise man when he moved the capital of Israel from Shechem, an indefensible site, commanded by overhanging mountains and approached by two easy vales, to Shomron, the "watch-hill" which stands in the centre of the broad Vale of Barley.

As we ride across the smiling corn-fields toward the isolated eminence, we see its strength as well as its beauty. It rises steeply from the valley to a height of more than three hundred feet. The encircling mountains are too far away to dominate it under the ancient conditions of warfare without cannons, and a good wall must have made it, as its name implied, an impregnable "stronghold," watching over a region of immense fertility.

What pomps and splendours, what revels and massacres, what joys of victory and horrors of defeat, that round hill rising from the Vale of Barley has seen. Now there is nothing left of its crown of pride, but the broken pillars of the marble colonnade a mile long with which Herod the Great girdled the hill, and a few indistinguishable ruins of the temple which he built in honour of the divine Augustus and of the hippodrome which he erected for the people. We climb the terraces and ride through the olive-groves and ploughed fields where the street of columns once ran. A few of them are standing upright; others leaning or fallen, half sunken in the ground; fragments of others built into the stone walls which divide the fields. There are many hewn and carven stones imbedded in the miserable little modern village which crouches on the north end of the hill, and the mosque into which the Crusaders' Church of Saint John has been transformed is said to contain the tombs of Elisha, Obadiah and John the Baptist. This rumour does not concern us deeply and we will leave its truth uninvestigated.

Let us tie our horses among Herod's pillars, and

spread the rugs for our noontide rest by the ruined south gate of the city. At our feet lies the wide, level, green valley where the mighty host of Benhadad, King of Damascus, once besieged the starving city and waited for its surrender. (II Kings vii.) There in the twilight of long ago a panic terror whispered through the camp, and the Syrians rose and fled, leaving their tents and their gear behind them. And there four nameless lepers of Israel, wandering in their despair, found the vast encampment deserted, and entered in, and ate and drank, and picked up gold and silver, until their conscience smote them. Then they climbed up to this gate with the good news that the enemy had vanished, and the city was saved.

IV

DÔTHÂN AND THE GOODNESS OF THE SAMARITAN

OVER the steep mountains that fence Samaria to the north, down through terraced vales abloom with hawthorns and blood-red poppies, across hill-circled plains where the long, silvery wind-waves roll over the sea of grain from shore to shore, past little gray towns sleeping on the sunny heights, by paths that lead us near flowing springs where the village girls fill their pitchers, and down stony slopes where the goatherds in bright-coloured raiment tend their flocks, and over broad, moist fields where the path has been obliterated by the plough, and around the edge of marshes where the storks rise heavily on long flapping wings, we come galloping at sunset to our camp beside the little green hill of Dôthân.

Behind it are the mountains, swelling and softly rounded like breasts. It was among them that the servant of Elisha saw the vision of horses and chariots of fire protecting his master. (II Kings vi: 14–19.)

North and east of Dôthân the plain extends smooth and gently sloping, full of young harvest. There the chariot of Naaman rolled when he came down from Damascus to be healed by the prophet of Israel. (II Kings v : 9.)

On top of the hill is a spreading terebinth-tree, with some traces of excavation and rude ruins beneath it. There Joseph's envious brethren cast him into one of the dry pits, from which they drew him up again to sell him to a caravan of merchants, winding across the plain on their way from Midian into Egypt. (Genesis xxxvii.)

Truly, many and wonderful things came to pass of old around this little green hill. And now, at the foot of it, there is a well-watered garden, with figs, oranges, almonds, vines, and tall, trembling poplars, surrounded by a hedge of prickly pear. Outside of the hedge a big, round spring of crystal water is flowing steadily over the rim of its basin of stones. There the flocks and herds are gathered, morning and evening, to drink. There the children of the tiny hamlet on the hillside come to paddle their feet in the running stream. There a caravan of Greek pilgrims, on their way from Damascus to Jerusalem for Easter, halt in front of our camp, to refresh themselves with a draught of the cool water.

As we watch them from our tents there is a sudden commotion among them, a cry of pain, and then voices of dismay. George and two or three of our men run out to see what is the matter, and come hurrying back to get some cotton cloth and oil and wine. One of the pilgrims, an old woman of seventy, has fallen from her horse on the sharp stones beside the spring, breaking her wrist and cutting her head.

I do not know whether the way in which they bound up that poor old stranger's wounds was surgically wise, but I know that it was humanly kind and tender. I do not know which of our various churches were represented among her helpers, but there must have been at least three, and the muleteer from Bagdad who "had no religion but sang beautiful Persian songs" was also there, and ready to help with the others. And so the parable which lighted our dusty way going down to Jericho is interpreted in our pleasant camp at Dôthân.

THE MOUNTAINS OF SAMARIA

The paths of the Creeds are many and winding; they cross and diverge; but on all of them the Good Samaritan is welcome, and I think he travels to a happy place.

A PSALM OF THE HELPERS

The ways of the world are full of haste and turmoil:
I will sing of the tribe of helpers who travel in peace.

He that turneth from the road to rescue another,
Turneth toward his goal:
He shall arrive in due time by the foot-path of mercy,
God will be his guide.

He that taketh up the burden of the fainting,
Lighteneth his own load:
The Almighty will put his arms underneath him,
He shall lean upon the Lord.

He that speaketh comfortable words to mourners,
Healeth his own heart:
In his time of grief they will return to remembrance,
God will use them for balm.

He that careth for the sick and wounded,
Watcheth not alone:
There are three in the darkness together,
And the third is the Lord.

Blessed is the way of the helpers:
The companions of the Christ.

X

GALILEE AND THE LAKE

I

THE PLAIN OF ESDRAELON

GOING from Samaria into Galilee is like passing from the Old Testament into the New.

There is indeed little difference in the outward landscape: the same bare lines of rolling mountains, green and gray near by, blue or purple far away; the same fertile valleys and emerald plains embosomed among the hills; the same orchards of olive-trees, not quite so large, nor so many, but always softening and shading the outlook with their touches of silvery verdure.

It is the spirit of the landscape that changes; the inward view; the atmosphere of memories and associations through which we travel. We have been riding with fierce warriors and proud kings and fiery prophets of Israel, passing the sites of royal splendour and fields of ancient havoc, retracing the warpaths of the Twelve Tribes. But when we enter Galilee the keynote of our thoughts is modulated into peace. Issachar and Zebulon and Asher and Naphtali have left no trace or message for us on the plains and hills where they once lived and fought. We journey with Jesus of Nazareth, the friend of publicans and sinners, the shepherd of the lost sheep, the human embodiment of the Divine Love.

This transition in our journey is marked outwardly by the crossing of the great Plain of Esdraelon, which we enter by the gateway of Jenîn. There are a few palm-trees lending a little grace to the disconsolate village, and the Turkish captain of the military post, a grizzled veteran of Plevna, invites us into the guard-room to drink coffee with him, while we wait for a dilatory telegraph operator to send a message. Then we push out upon the green sea to a brown island: the village of Zer'în, the ancient Jezreel.

The wretched hamlet of adobe huts, with mud beehives plastered against the walls, stands on the lowest bench of the foothills of Mount Gilboa, opposite the equally wretched hamlet of Sûlem in a corresponding position at the base of a mountain called Little Hermon. The widespread, opulent view is haunted with old stories of battle, murder and sudden death.

Down to the east we see the line of brighter green creeping out from the flanks of Mount Gilboa, marking the spring where Gideon sifted his band of warriors for the night-attack on the camp of Midian. (Judges vii : 4–23.) Under the brow of the hill are the ancient wine-presses, cut in the rock, which belonged to the vineyard of Naboth, whom Jezebel assassinated. (I Kings xxi: 1–16.) From some window of her favourite palace on this eminence, that hard, old, painted queen looked down the broad valley of Jezreel, and saw Jehu in his chariot driving furiously from Gilead to bring vengeance upon her. On those dark ridges to the south the brave Jonathan was slain by the Philistines and the desperate Saul fell upon his own sword. (I Samuel xxxi: 1–6.) Through that open valley, which slopes so gently down to the Jordan at Bethshan, the hordes of Midian and the hosts of Damascus marched against Israel. By the pass of Jenîn, Holofernes led his army in triumph until he met Judith of Bethulia and lost his head. Yonder in the corner to the northward, at the base of Mount Tabor, Deborah and Barak gathered the tribes against the Canaanites under Sisera. (Judges iv: 4–22.) Away to the westward, in the notch of Megiddo, Pharaoh-Necho's archers pierced King Josiah, and there was great mourning for him in Hadad-rimmon. (II Chronicles xxxv: 24–25; Zechariah xii: 11.) Farther still, where the mountain spurs of Galilee approach the long ridge of Carmel, Elijah put the priests of Baal to death by the Brook Kishon. (I Kings xviii: 20–40.)

All over that great prairie, which makes a broad break between the highlands of Galilee and the highlands of Samaria and Judea, and opens an easy pathway rising no more than three hundred feet between the Jordan and the Mediterranean—all over that fertile, blooming area and around the edges of it are sown the legends

> "Of old, unhappy, far-off things
> And battles long ago."

But on this bright April day when we enter the plain of Armageddon, everything is tranquil and joyous.

The fields are full of rustling wheat, and bearded barley, and blue-green stalks of beans, and feathery *kirsenneh*, camel-provender. The peasants in their gay-coloured clothing are ploughing the rich, red-brown soil for the late crop of *doura*. The newly built railway from Haifa to Damascus lies like a yellow string across the prairie from west to east; and from north to south a single file of two hundred camels, with merchandise for Egypt, undulate along the ancient road of the caravans, turning their ungainly heads to look at the puffing engine which creeps toward them from the distance.

Larks singing in the air, storks parading beside the watercourses, falcons poising overhead, poppies and pink gladioluses and blue corn-cockles blooming through the grain,—a little village on a swell of rising ground, built for their farm hands by the rich Greeks who have bought the land and brought it under cultivation,—an air so pure and soft that it is like a caress,—all seems to speak a language of peace and promise, as if one of the old prophets were telling of the day when Jehovah shall have compassion on His people Israel and restore them. "They that dwell under His shadow shall return; they shall revive as the grain, and blossom as the vine: the scent thereof shall be as the wine of Lebanon."

It is, indeed, not impossible that wise methods of colonization, better agriculture and gardening, the development of fruit-orchards and vineyards, and above all, more rational government and equitable taxation may one day give back to Palestine something of her old prosperity and population. If the Jews really want it no doubt they can have it. Their rich men have the money and the influence; and there are enough of their poorer folk scattered through Europe to make any land blossom like the rose, if they have the will and the patience for the slow toil of the husbandman and the vine-dresser and the shepherd and the herdsman.

But the proud kingdom of David and Solomon will never be restored; not even the tributary kingdom of Herod. For the land will never again stand at the crossroads, the four-corners of the civilized world. The Suez Canal to the south, and the railways through the Lebanon and Asia Minor to the north, have settled that. They have left Palestine in a corner, off the main-travelled roads. The best that she can hope for is a restoration to quiet fruitfulness, to placid and humble industry, to olive-crowned and vine-girdled felicity, never again to power.

And if that lowly re-coronation comes to her, it will not be on the stony heights around Jerusalem: it will be in the Plain of Sharon, in the outgoings of Mount Ephraim, in the green pastures of Gilead, in the lovely region of "Galilee of the Gentiles." It will not be by the sword of Gideon nor by the sceptre of Solomon, but by the sign of peace on earth and good-will among men.

With thoughts like these we make our way across the verdurous inland sea of Esdraelon, out of the Old Testament into the New. Landmarks of the country of the Gospel begin to appear: the wooded dome of Mount Tabor, the little village of Nain where Jesus restored the widow's only son. (Luke vii: 11–16.) But these lie far to our right. The beacon which guides us is a glimpse of white walls and red roofs, high on a shoulder of the Galilean hills: the outlying houses of Nazareth, where the boy Jesus dwelt with His parents after their return from the flight into Egypt, and was obedient to them, and grew in wisdom and stature, and in favour with God and men.

II

THEIR OWN CITY NAZARETH

Our camp in Nazareth is on a terrace among the olive-trees, on the eastern side of a small valley, facing the Mohammedan quarter of the town.

This is distinctly the most attractive little city that we have seen in Palestine. The houses are spread out over a wider area than is usual in the East, covering three sides of a gentle depression high on the side of the Jebel es-Sikh, and creeping up the hill-slopes as if to seek a larger view and a purer air. Some of them have gardens, fair white walls, red-tiled roofs, balconies of stone or wrought iron. Even in the more closely built portion of the town the streets seem cleaner, the bazaars lighter and less malodorous, the interior courtyards into which we glance in passing more neat and homelike. Many of the doorways and living-rooms of the humbler houses are freshly whitewashed with a light-blue tint which gives them an immaculate air of cleanliness.

The Nazarene women are generally good looking, and free and dignified in their bearing. The children, fairer in complexion than is common in Syria, are almost all charming with the beauty of youth, and among them are some very lovely faces of boys and girls. I do not mean to say that Nazareth appears to us an earthly paradise; only that it shines by contrast with places like Hebron and Jericho and Nablûs, even with Bethlehem, and that we find here far less of human squalor and misery to sadden us with thoughts of

"What man has made of man."

The population of the town is about eleven or twelve thousand, a quarter of them Mussulmans, and the rest Christians of various sects, including two or three hundred Protestants. The people used to have rather a bad reputation for turbulence; but we see no signs of it, either in the appearance of the city or in the demeanour of the inhabitants. The children and the townsfolk whom we meet in the streets, and of whom we ask our way now and then, are civil and friendly. The man who comes to the camp to sell us antique coins and lovely vases of iridescent glass dug from the tombs of Tyre and Sidon, may be an inveterate humbug, but his manners are good and his prices are low. The soft-voiced women and lustrous-eyed girls who hang about the Lady's tent, persuading her to buy their small embroideries and lace-work and trinkets, are gentle and ingratiating, though persistent.

I am honestly of the opinion that Christian mission-schools and hospitals have done a great deal for Nazareth. We go this morning to visit the schools of the English Church Missionary Society, where Miss Newton is conducting an admirable and most successful work for the girls of Nazareth. She is away on a visit to some of her outlying stations; but the dark-eyed, happy-looking Syrian teacher shows us all the classes. There are five of them, and every room is full and bright and orderly.

On the Christian side, the older girls sing a hymn for us, in their high voices and quaint English accent, about Jesus stilling the storm on Galilee, and the intermediate girls and the tiny co-educated boys and girls in the kindergarten go through various pretty performances. Then the teacher leads us across the street to the two Moslem classes, and we cannot tell the difference between them and the Christian children, except that now the singing of "Jesus loves me" and the recitation of "The Lord is my Shepherd" are in Arabic. There is one blind girl who recites most perfectly and eagerly. Another girl of about ten years carries her baby-brother in her arms. Two little laggards, (they were among the group at our camp early in the morning), arrive late, weeping out their excuses to the teacher. She hears them with a kind, humorous look on her face, gives them a soft rebuke and a task, and sends them to their seats, their tears suddenly transformed to smiles.

From the schools we go to the hospital of the British Medical Mission, a little higher up the hill. We find young Doctor Scrimgeour, who has lately come out from Edinburgh University, and his white-uniformed, cheerful, busy nurses, tasked to the limit of their strength by the pressure of their work, but cordial and simple in their welcome. As I walk with the doctor on his rounds I see every ward full, and all kinds of calamity and suffering waiting for the relief and help of his kind, skilful knife. Here are hernia, and tuberculous glands, and cataract, and stone, and bone tuberculosis, and a score of other miseries; and there, on the table, with pale, dark face and mysterious eyes, lies a man whose knee has been shattered by a ball from a Martini rifle in an affray with robbers.

"Was he one of the robbers," I ask, "or one of the robbed?"

"I really don't know," says the doctor, "but in a few minutes I am going to do my best for him."

Is not this Christ's work that is still doing in Christ's town, this teaching of the children, this helping of the sick and wounded, for His sake, and in His name? Yet there are silly folk who say they do not believe in missions.

There are a few so-called sacred places and shrines in Nazareth—the supposed scene of the Annunciation; the traditional Workshop of Joseph; the alleged *Mensa Christi*, a flat stone which He is said to have used as a table when He ate with His disciples; and so on. But all these uncertain relics and memorials, as usual, are inclosed in chapels, belit with lamps, and encircled with ceremonial. The very spring at which the Virgin Mary must have often filled her pitcher, (for it is the only flowing fountain in the town), now rises beneath the Greek Church of Saint Gabriel, and is conducted past the altar in a channel of stone where the pilgrims bathe their eyes and faces. To us, who are seeking our Holy Land out-of-doors, these shut-in shrines and altared memorials are less significant than what we find in the open, among the streets and on the surrounding hillsides.

The Virgin's Fountain, issuing from the church, flows into a big, stone basin under a round arch. Here, as often as we pass, we see the maidens and the mothers of Nazareth, with great earthern vessels poised upon their shapely heads, coming with merry talk and laughter, to draw water. Even so the mother of Jesus must have come to this fountain many a time, perhaps with her wondrous boy running beside her, clasping her hand or a fold of her bright-coloured garment. Perhaps, when the child was little she carried Him on her shoulder, as the women carry their children to-day.

Passing through a street, we look into the interior of a carpenter-shop, with its simple tools, its little pile of new lumber, its floor littered with chips and shavings, and its air full of the pleasant smell of freshly cut wood. There are a few articles of furniture which the carpenter has made: a couple of chairs, a table, a stool: and he himself, with his leg stretched out and his piece of wood held firmly by his naked toes, is working busily at a tiny bed which needs only a pair of rockers to become a cradle. Outside the door of the shop a boy of ten or twelve is cutting some boards and slats, and putting them neatly together. We ask him what he is making. "A box," he answers, "a box for some doves"—and then bends his head over his absorbing task. Even so Jesus must have worked at the shop of Joseph, the carpenter, and learned His handicraft.

Let us walk up, at eventide, to the top of the hill behind the town. Here is one of the loveliest views in all Palestine. The sun is setting and the clear-

The Virgin's Fountain, Nazareth.

obscure of twilight already rests over the streets and houses, the minarets and spires, the slender cypresses and round olive-trees and grotesque hedges of cactus. But on the heights the warm radiance from the west pours its full flood, lighting up all the flowerets of delicate pink flax and golden chrysanthemum and blue campanula with which the grass is broidered. Far and wide that roseate illumination spreads itself; changing the snowy mantle of distant Hermon, the great Sheikh of Mountains, from ermine to flamingo feathers; making the high hills of Naphtali and the excellency of Carmel glow as if with soft, transfiguring, inward fire; touching the little town of Saffû-riyeh below us, where they say that the Virgin Mary was born, and the city of Safed, thirty miles away on the lofty shoulder of Jebel Jermak; suffusing the haze that fills the Valley of the Jordan, and the long bulwarks of the Other-Side, with hues of mauve and purple; and bathing the wide expanse of the western sea with indescribable splendours, over which the flaming sun poises for a moment beneath the edge of a low-hung cloud.

On this hilltop, I doubt not, the boy Jesus often

filled His hands with flowers. Here He could watch the creeping caravans of Arabian merchants, and the glittering legions of Roman soldiers, and the slow files of Jewish pilgrims, coming up from the Valley of Jezreel and stretching out across the Plain of Esdraelon. Hither, at the evening hour, He came as a youth to find the blessing of wide and tranquil thought. Here, when the burden of manhood pressed upon Him, He rested after the day's work, free from that sadness which often touches us in the vision of earth's transient beauty, because He saw far beyond the horizon into the spirit-world, where there is no night, nor weariness, nor sin, nor death.

For nearly thirty years He must have lived within sight of this hilltop. And then, one day, He came back from a journey to the Jordan and Jerusalem, and entered into the little synagogue at the foot of this hill, and began to preach to His townsfolk His glad tidings of spiritual liberty and brotherhood and eternal life.

But they were filled with scorn and wrath. His words rebuked them, stung them, inflamed them with hatred. They laid violent hands on Him, and led Him out to the brow of the hill,—perhaps it was yonder on that steep, rocky peak to the south of the town, looking back toward the country of the Old Testament,—to cast Him down headlong.

Yet I think there must have been a few friends and lovers of His in that disdainful and ignorant crowd; for He passed through the midst of them unharmed, and went His way to the home of Peter and Andrew and John and Philip, beside the Sea of Galilee, never to come back to Nazareth.

III

A WEDDING IN CANA OF GALILEE

We thought to save a little time on our journey, and perhaps to spare ourselves a little jolting on the hard high-road, by sending the saddle-horses ahead with the caravan, and taking a carriage for the sixteen-mile drive to Tiberias. When we came to the old sarcophagus which serves as a drinking trough at the spring outside the village of Cana, a strange thing befell us.

We had halted for a moment to refresh the horses.

Suddenly there was a sound of furious galloping on the road behind us. A score of cavaliers in Bedouin dress, with guns and swords, came after us in hot haste. The leaders dashed across the open space beside the spring, wheeled their foaming horses and dashed back again.

"Is this our affair with robbers, at last?" we asked George.

He laughed a little. "No," said he, "this is the beginning of a wedding in Kafr Kennâ. The bridegroom and his friends come over from some other village where they live, to show off a bit of *fantasia* to the bride and her friends. They carry her back with them after the marriage. We wait a while and see how they ride."

The horses were gayly caparisoned with ribbons and tassels and embroidered saddle-cloths. The riders were handsome, swarthy fellows with haughty faces. Their eyes glanced sideways at us to see whether we were admiring them, as they shouted their challenges to one another and raced wildly up and down the rock-strewn course, with their robes flying and their horses' sides bloody with spurring. One of the men was a huge coal-black Nubian who brandished a naked sword as he rode. Others whirled their long muskets in the air and yelled furiously. The riding was cruel, reckless, superb; loose reins and loose stirrups on the headlong gallop; then the sharp curb brought the horse up suddenly, the rein on his neck turned him as if on a pivot, and the pressure of the heel sent him flying back over the course.

Presently there was a sound of singing and clapping hands behind the high cactus-hedges to our left, and from a little lane the bridal procession walked up to take the high-road to the village. There were a dozen men in front, firing guns and shouting, then came the women, with light veils of gauze over their faces, singing shrilly, and in the midst of them, in gay attire, but half-concealed with long, dark mantles, the bride and "the virgins, her companions, in raiment of needlework."

As they saw the photographic camera pointed at them they laughed, and crowded closer together, and drew the ends of their dark mantles over their heads. So they passed up the road, their shrill song broken a little by their laughter; and the company of horsemen, the bridegroom and his friends, wheeled into line, two by two, and trotted after them into the village.

This was all that we saw of the wedding at Kafr Kennâ—just a vivid, mysterious flash of human figures, drawn together by the primal impulse and longing of our common nature, garbed and ordered by the social customs which make different lands and ages seem strange to each other, and moving across the narrow stage of Time into the dimness of that Arab village, where Jesus and His mother and His disciples were guests at a wedding long ago.

IV

TIBERIAS

It is one of the ironies of fate that the lake which saw the greater part of the ministry of Jesus, should take its modern name from a city built by Herod Antipas, and called after one of the most infamous of the Roman Emperors,—"the Sea of Tiberias."

Our road to this city of decadence leads gradually

downward, through a broad, sinking moorland, covered with weeds and wild flowers—rich, monotonous, desolate. The broidery of pink flax and yellow chrysanthemums and white marguerites still follows us; but now the wider stretches of thistles and burdocks and daturas and cockleburs and water-plantains seem to be more important. The landscape saddens around us, under the deepening haze of the desert-wind, the sombre Sherkîyeh. There are no golden sunbeams, no cool cloud-shadows, only a gray and melancholy illumination growing ever fainter and more nebulous as the day declines, and the outlines of the hills fade away from the dim, silent, forsaken plain through which we move.

We are crossing the battlefield where the soldiers of Napoleon, under the brave Junot, fought desperately against the overwhelming forces of the Turks. Yonder, away to the left, in the mysterious haze, the double "Horns of Hattin" rise like a shadowy exhalation.

That is said to be the mountain where Jesus gathered the multitude around Him and spoke His new beatitudes on the meek, the merciful, the peacemakers, the pure in heart. It is certainly the place where the hosts of the Crusaders met the army of Saladin, in the fierce heat of a July day, seven hundred years ago, and while the burning grass and weeds and brush flamed around them, were cut to pieces and trampled and utterly consumed. There the new Kingdom of Jerusalem,—the last that was won with the sword,—went down in ruin around the relics of "the true cross," which its soldiers carried as their talisman; and Guy de Lusignan, their King, was captured. The noble prisoners were invited by Saladin to his tent, and he offered them sherbets, cooled with snow from Hermon, to slake their feverish thirst. When they were refreshed, the conqueror ordered them to be led out and put to the sword,—just yonder at the foot of the Mount of Beatitudes.

From terrace to terrace of the falling moor we roll along the winding road through the brumous twilight, until we come within sight of the black, ruined walls, the gloomy towers, the huddled houses of the worn-out city of Tiberias. She is like an ancient beggar sitting on a rocky cape beside the lake and bathing her feet in the invisible water. The gathering dusk lends a sullen and forlorn aspect to the place. Behind us rise the shattered volcanic crags and cliffs of basalt; before us glimmer pallid and ghostly touches of light from the hidden waves; a few lamps twinkle here and there in the dormant town.

This was the city which Herod Antipas built for the capital of his Province of Galilee. He laid its foundations in an ancient graveyard, and stretched its walls three miles along the lake, adorning it with a palace, a forum, a race-course, and a large synagogue. But to strict Jews the place was unclean, because it was defiled with Roman idols, and because its builders had polluted themselves by digging up the bones of the dead. Herod could get few Jews to live in his city, and it became a catch-all for the off-scourings of the land, people of all creeds and none, aliens, mongrels, soldiers of fortune, and citizens of the high-road. It was the strongest fortress and probably the richest town of Galilee in Christ's day, but so far as we know He never entered it.

After the fall of Jerusalem, strangely enough, the Jews made it their favourite city, the seat of their

Sanhedrim and the centre of rabbinical learning. Here the famous Rabbis Jehuda and Akîba and the philosopher Maimonides taught. Here the Mishna and the Gemara were written. And here, to-day, two-thirds of the five thousand inhabitants are Jews, many of them living on the charity of their kindred in Europe, and spending their time in the study of the Talmud while they wait for the Messiah who shall restore the kingdom to Israel. You may see their flat fur caps, dingy gabardines, long beards and melancholy faces on every street in the drowsy little city, dreaming (among fleas and fevers) of I know not what impossible glories to come.

You may see, also, on the hill near the Serai, the splendid Mission Hospital of the United Free Church of Scotland, where for twenty-three years Doctor Torrance has been ministering to the body and soul of Tiberias in the name of Jesus. Do you find the building too large and fine, the lovely garden too beautiful with flowers, the homes of the doctors, and teachers, and helpers of the sick and wounded, too clean and healthful and orderly? Do you say "To what purpose is this waste?" Then I know not how to measure your ignorance. For you have failed to see that this is the embassy of the only King who still cares for the true welfare of this forsaken, bedraggled, broken-down Tiberias.

On the evening of our arrival, however, all these things are hidden from us in the dusk. We drive past the ruined gate of the city, a mile along the southern road toward the famous Hot Baths. Here, on a little terrace above the lake, between the road and the black basalt cliffs, our camp is pitched, and through the darkness

> 'We hear the water lapping on the crag,
> And the long ripple washing in the reeds.'

In the freshness of the early morning the sunrise pours across the lake into our tents. There is a light, cool breeze blowing from the north, rippling the clear, green water, (of a hue like the stone called *aqua marina*), with a thousand flaws and wrinkles, which catch the flashing light and reflect the deep blue sky, and change beneath the shadow of floating clouds to innumerable colours of lapis lazuli, and violet, and purple, and peacock blue.

The old comparison of the shape of the lake to a lute, or a harp, is not clear to us from the point at which we stand: for the northwestward sweep of the bay of Gennesaret, which reaches a breadth of nearly eight miles from the eastern shore, is hidden from us by a promontory, where the dark walls and white houses of Tiberias slope to the water. But we can see the full length of the lake, from the depression of the Jordan Valley at the southern end, to the shores of Bethsaida and Capernaum at the foot of the northern hills, beyond which the dazzling whiteness of Hermon is visible.

Opposite rise the eastern heights of the Jaulân, with almost level top and steep flanks, furrowed by rocky ravines, descending precipitously to a strip of smooth, green shore. Behind us the mountains are more broken and varied in form, lifted into sharper peaks and sloped into broader valleys. The whole aspect of the scene is like a view in the English Lake country, say on Windermere or Ullswater; only there are no forests or thickets to shade and soften it. Every edge of the hills is like a silhouette against the sky; every curve of the shore clear and distinct.

Of the nine rich cities which once surrounded the lake, none is left except this ragged old Tiberias. Of the hundreds of fishing boats and passenger vessels which once crossed its waters, all have vanished except half a dozen little pleasure skiffs kept for the use of tourists. Of the armies and caravans which once travelled these shores, all have passed by into the eternal far-away, except the motley string of visitors to the Hot Springs, who were coming up to bathe in the medicinal waters in the days of Joshua when the place was called Hammath, and in the time of the Greeks when it was named Emmaus, and who are still trotting along the road in front of our camp toward the big, white dome and dirty bath-houses of Hummam. They come from all parts of Syria, from Damascus and the sea-coast, from Judea and the Haurân; Greeks and Arabs and Turks and Maronites and Jews; on foot, on donkey-back, and in litters. Now, it is a cavalcade of Druses from the Lebanon, men, women and children, riding on tired horses. Now, it is a procession of Hebrews walking with a silken canopy over the sacred books of their law.

GALILEE AND THE LAKE

In the morning we visit Tiberias, buy some bread and fish in the market, and go through the Mission Hospital, where one of the gentle nurses binds up a foolish little wound on my wrist.

In the afternoon we sail on the southern part of the lake. The boatmen laugh at my fruitless fishing with artificial flies, and catch a few small fish for us with their nets in the shallow, muddy places along the shore. The wind is strange and variable, now sweeping down in violent gusts that bend the long arm of the lateen sail, now dying away to a dead calm through which we row lazily home.

I remember a small purple kingfisher poising in the air over a shoal, his head bent downward, his wings vibrating swiftly. He drops like a shot and comes up out of the water with a fish held crosswise in his bill. With measured wing-strokes he flits to the top of a rock to eat his supper, and a robber-gull flaps after him to take it away. But the industrious kingfisher is too quick to be robbed. He bolts his fish with a single gulp. We eat ours in more leisurely fashion, by the light of the candles in our peaceful tent.

V

MEMORIES OF THE LAKE

A HUNDRED little points of illumination flash into memory as I look back over the hours that we spent beside the Sea of Galilee. How should I write of them all without being tedious? How, indeed, should I hope to make them visible or significant in the bare words of description?

Never have I passed richer, fuller hours; but most of their wealth was in very little things: the personal look of a flower growing by the wayside; the intimate message of a bird's song falling through the sunny air; the expression of confidence and appeal on the face of a wounded man in the hospital, when the good physician stood beside his cot; the shadows of the mountains lengthening across the valleys at sunset; the laughter of a little child playing with a broken water pitcher; the bronzed profiles and bold, free ways of our sunburned rowers; the sad eyes of an old Hebrew lifted from the book that he was reading; the ruffling breezes and sudden squalls that changed the surface of the lake; the

247

single palm-tree that waved over the mud hovels of
Magdala; the millions of tiny shells that strewed
the beach of Capernaum and Bethsaida; the fertile sweep of the Plain of Gennesaret rising from
the lake; and the dark precipices of the "Robbers'
Gorge" running back into the western mountains.

The written record of these hours is worth little;
but in experience and in memory they have a mystical
meaning and beauty, because they belong to the
country where Jesus walked with His fishermen-
disciples, and took the little children in His arms,
and healed the sick, and opened blind eyes to behold
ineffable things.

Every touch that brings that country nearer to
us in our humanity and makes it more real, more
simple, more vivid, is precious. For the one irrep-
arable loss that could befall us in religion,—a loss
that is often threatened by our abstract and theo-
retical ways of thinking and speaking about Him,—
would be to lose Jesus out of the lowly and familiar
ways of our mortal life. He entered these lowly ways
as the Son of Man in order to make us sure that
we are the children of God.

Therefore I am glad of every hour spent by the Lake of Galilee.

I remember, when we came across in our boat to Tell Hûm, where the ancient city of Capernaum stood, the sun was shining with a fervent heat and the air of the lake, six hundred and eighty feet below the level of the sea, was soft and languid. The gray-bearded German monk who came to meet us at the landing and admitted us to the inclosure of his little monastery where he was conducting the excavation of the ruins, wore a cork helmet and spectacles. He had been heated, even above the ninety degrees Fahrenheit which the thermometer marked, by the rudeness of a couple of tourists who had just tried to steal a photograph of his work. He had foiled them by opening their camera and blotting the film with sunlight, and had then sent them away with fervent words. But as he walked with us among his roses and Pride of India trees, his spirit cooled within him, and he showed himself a learned and accomplished man.

He told us how he had been working there for two

or three years, keeping records and drawings and photographs of everything that was found; going back to the Franciscan convent at Jerusalem for his short vacation in the heat of mid-summer; putting his notes in order, reading and studying, making ready to write his book on Capernaum. He showed us the portable miniature railway which he had made; and the little iron cars to carry away the great piles of rubbish and earth; and the rich columns, carved lintels, marble steps and shell-niches of the splendid building which his workmen had uncovered. The outline was clear and perfect. We could see how the edifice of fine, white limestone had been erected upon an older foundation of basalt, and how an earthquake had twisted it and shaken down its pillars. It was undoubtedly a synagogue, perhaps the very same which the rich Roman centurion built for the Jews in Capernaum (Luke vii: 5), and where Jesus healed the man who had an unclean spirit. (Luke iv: 31–37.) Of all the splendours of that proud city of the lake, once spreading along a mile of the shore, nothing remained but these tumbled ruins in a lonely, fragrant garden, where the patient father was digging with his Arab workmen and getting ready to write his book.

"*Weh dir, Capernaum*" I quoted. The *padre* nodded his head gravely. "*Ja, ja,*" said he, "*es ist buchstäblich erfüllt!*"

I remember the cool bath in the lake, at a point between Bethsaida and Capernaum, where a tangle of briony and honeysuckle made a shelter around a shell-strewn beach, and the rosy oleanders bloomed beside an inflowing stream. I swam out a little way and floated, looking up into the deep sky, while the waves plashed gently and caressingly around my face.

I remember the old Arab fisherman, who was camped with his family in a black tent on a meadow where several lively brooks came in (one of them large enough to turn a mill). I persuaded him by gestures to wade out into the shallow part of the lake and cast his bell-net for fish. He gathered the net in his hand, and whirled it around his head. The leaden weights around the bottom spread out in a wide circle and splashed into the water. He drew the net toward him by the cord, the ring of sinkers

sweeping the bottom, and lifted it slowly, carefully—
but no fish!

Then I rigged up my pocket fly-rod with a gossa-
mer leader and two tiny trout-flies, a Royal Coach-
man and a Queen of the Water, and began to cast
along the crystal pools and rapids of the larger
stream. How merrily the fish rose there, and in the
ripples where the brooks ran out into the lake. There
were half a dozen different kinds of fish, but I did
not know the name of any of them. There was one
that looked like a black bass, and others like white
perch and sunfish; and one kind was very much like
a grayling. But they were not really of the *salmo*
family, I knew, for none of them had the soft fin in
front of the tail. How surprised the old fisherman
was when he saw the fish jumping at those tiny hooks
with feathers; and how round the eyes of his children were as they looked on; and how pleased they
were with the *bakhshîsh* which they received, including a couple of baithooks for the eldest boy!

I remember the place where we ate our lunch in
a small grove of eucalyptus-trees, with sweet-smell-

ing yellow acacias blossoming around us. It was near the site which some identify with the ancient Bethsaida, but others say that it was farther to the east, and others again say that Capernaum was really located here. The whole problem of these lake cities, where they stood, how they supported such large populations (not less than fifteen thousand people in each), is difficult and may never be solved. But it did not trouble us deeply. We were content to be beside the same waters, among the same hills, that Jesus knew and loved.

It was here, along this shore, that He found Simon and his brother Andrew casting their net, and James and his brother John mending theirs, and called them to come with Him. These fishermen, with their frank and free hearts unspoiled by the sophistries of the Pharisees, with their minds unhampered by social and political ambitions, followers of a vocation which kept them out of doors and reminded them daily of their dependence on the bounty of God,—these children of nature, and others like them, were the men whom He chose for His disciples, the listeners who had ears to hear His marvellous gospel.

It was here, on these pale, green waves, that He sat in a little boat, near the shore, and spoke to the multitude who had gathered to hear Him.

He spoke of the deep and tranquil confidence that man may learn from nature, from the birds and the flowers.

He spoke of the infinite peace of the heart that knows the true meaning of love, which is giving and blessing, and the true secret of courage, which is loyalty to the truth.

He spoke of the God whom we can trust as a child trusts its father, and of the Heaven which waits for all who do good to their fellowmen.

He spoke of the wisdom whose fruit is not pride but humility, of the honour whose crown is not authority but service, of the purity which is not outward but inward, and of the joy which lasts forever.

He spoke of forgiveness for the guilty, of compassion for the weak, of hope for the desperate.

He told these poor and lowly folk that their souls were unspeakably precious, and that He had come to save them and make them inheritors of an eternal kingdom. He told them that He had brought this message from God, their Father and His Father.

He spoke with the simplicity of one who knows, with the assurance of one who has seen, with the certainty and clearness of one for whom doubt does not exist.

He offered Himself, in His stainless purity, in His supreme love, as the proof and evidence of His gospel, the bread of Heaven, the water of life, the Saviour of sinners, the light of the world. "Come unto Me," He said, "and I will give you rest."

This was the heavenly music that came into the world by the Lake of Galilee. And its voice has spread through the centuries, comforting the sorrowful, restoring the penitent, cheering the despondent, and telling all who will believe it, that our human life is worth living, because it gives each one of us the opportunity to share in the Love which is sovereign and immortal.

A PSALM OF THE GOOD TEACHER

The Lord is my teacher:
I shall not lose the way to wisdom.

He leadeth me in the lowly path of learning,
He prepareth a lesson for me every day;
He findeth the clear fountains of instruction,
Little by little he showeth me the beauty of the truth.

The world is a great book that he hath written,
He turneth the leaves for me slowly;
They are all inscribed with images and letters,
His face poureth light on the pictures and the words

Then am I glad when I perceive his meaning,
He taketh me by the hand to the hill-top of vision;
In the valley also he walketh beside me,
And in the dark places he whispereth to my heart.

Yea, though my lesson be hard it is not hopeless,
For the Lord is very patient with his slow scholar;
He will wait awhile for my weakness,
He will help me to read the truth through tears.

*Surely thou wilt enlighten me daily by joy and by
sorrow:
And lead me at last, O Lord, to the perfect knowledge
of thee.*

XI

THE SPRINGS OF JORDAN

I

THE HILL-COUNTRY OF NAPHTALI

NAPHTALI was the northernmost of the tribes of Israel, a bold and free highland clan, inhabiting a country of rugged hills and steep mountainsides, with fertile vales and little plains between.

"Naphtali is a hind let loose," said the old song of the Sons of Jacob (Genesis xlix: 21); and as we ride up from the Lake of Galilee on our way northward, we feel the meaning of the poet's words. A people dwelling among these rock-strewn heights, building their fortress-towns on sharp pinnacles, and climbing these steep paths to the open fields of tillage or of war, would be like wild deer in their spirit of liberty, and they would need to be as nimble and sure-footed.

Our good little horses are shod with round plates of iron, and they clatter noisily among the loose stones and slip on the rocky ledges, as we strike over the hills from Capernaum, without a path, to join the main trail at Khân Yubb Yûsuf.

We are skirting fields of waving wheat and barley, but there are no houses to be seen. Far and wide the sea of verdure rolls around us, broken only by ridges of grayish rock and scarped cliffs of reddish basalt. We wade saddle-deep in herbage; broad-leaved fennel and trembling reeds; wild asparagus and artichokes; a hundred kinds of flowering weeds; acres of last year's thistles, standing blanched and ghostlike in the summer sunshine.

The phantom city of Safed gleams white from its far-away hilltop,—the latest and perhaps the last of the famous seats of rabbinical learning. It is one of the sacred places of modern Judaism. No Hebrew pilgrim fails to visit it. Here, they say, the Messiah will one day reveal himself, and after establishing His kingdom, will set out to conquer the world.

But it is not to the city, shining like a flake of mica from the greenness of the distant mountain, that our looks and thoughts are turning. It is backward to the lucent sapphire of the Lake of Galilee, upon whose shores our hearts have seen the secret vision, heard the inward message of the Man of Nazareth.

Ridge after ridge reveals new outlooks toward its tranquil loveliness. Turn after turn, our winding way leads us to what we think must be the parting view. Sleeping in still, forsaken beauty among the sheltering hills, and open to the cloudless sky which makes its water like a little heaven, it seems to silently return our farewell looks with pleading for remembrance. Now, after one more round among the inclosing ridges, another vista opens, the widest and the most serene of all.

Farewell, dear Lake of Jesus! Our eyes may never rest on thee again; but surely they will not forget thee. For now, as often we come to some fair water in the Western mountains, or unfold the tent by some lone lakeside in the forests of the North, the lapping of thy waves will murmur through our thoughts; thy peaceful brightness will arise before us; we shall see the rose-flush of thy oleanders, and the waving of thy reeds; the sweet, faint smell of thy gold-flowered acacias will return to us from purple orchids and white lilies. Let the blessing that is thine go with us everywhere in God's great out-of-doors, and our hearts never lose the comrade-

ship of Him who made thee holiest among all the
waters of the world!

The Khân of Joseph's Pit is a ruin; a huge and
broken building deserted by the caravans which
used to throng this highway from Damascus to the
cities of the lake, and to the ports of Acre and
Joppa, and to the metropolis of Egypt. It is hard
to realize that this wild moorland path by which we
are travelling was once a busy road, filled with camels, horses, chariots, foot-passengers, clanking companies of soldiers; that these crumbling, cavernous
walls, overgrown with thorny capers and wild marjoram and mandragora, were once crowded every
night with a motley mob of travellers and merchants;
that this pool of muddy water, gloomily reflecting
the ruins, was once surrounded by flocks and herds
and beasts of burden; that only a few hours to the
southward there was once a ring of splendid, thriving, bustling towns around the shores of Galilee,
out of which and into which the multitudes were
forever journeying. Now they are all gone from
the road, and the vast wayside caravanserai is

sleeping into decay—a dormitory for bats and serpents.

What is it that makes the wreck of an inn more lonely and forbidding than any other ruin?

A few miles more of riding along the flanks of the mountains bring us to a place where we turn a corner suddenly, and come upon the full view of the upper basin of the Jordan; a vast oval green cup, with the little Lake of Huleh lying in it like a blue jewel, and the giant bulk of Mount Hermon towering beyond it, crowned and cloaked with silver snows.

Up the steep and slippery village street of Rosh Pinnah, a modern Jewish colony founded by the Rothschilds in 1882, we scramble wearily to our camping-ground for the night. Above us on a hilltop is the old Arab village of Jaûneh, brown, picturesque, and filthy. Around us are the colonists' new houses, with their red-tiled roofs and white walls. Two straight streets running in parallel lines up the hillside are roughly paved with cobble-stones and lined with trees; mulberries, white-flowered acacias, eucalyptus, feathery pepper-trees, and rose-bushes. Water runs down through pipes from a copious spring on the mountain, and flows abundantly into every house, plashing into covered reservoirs and open stone basins for watering the cattle. Below us the long avenues of eucalyptus, the broad vineyards filled with low, bushy vines, the immense orchards of pale-green almond-trees, the smiling wheat-fields, slope to the lake and encircle its lower end.

The children who come to visit our camp on the terrace wear shoes and stockings, carry school-books in their bags, and bring us offerings of little bunches of sweet-smelling garden roses and pendulous locust-blooms. We are a thousand years away from the Khân of Joseph's Pit; but we can still see the old mud village on the height against the sunset, and the camp-fires gleaming in front of the black Bedouin tents far below, along the edge of the marshes. We are perched between the old and the new, between the nomad and the civilized man, and the unchanging white head of Hermon looks down upon us all.

In the morning, on the way down, I stop at the door of a house and fall into talk with an intelligent, schoolmasterish sort of man, a Roumanian, who speaks a little weird German. Is the colony prospering? Yes, but not so fast that it makes them giddy. What are they raising? Wheat and barley, a few vegetables, a great deal of almonds and grapes. Good harvests? Some years good, some years bad; the Arabs bad every year, terrible thieves; but the crops are plentiful most of the time. Are the colonists happy, contented? A thin smile wrinkles around the man's lips as he answers with the statement of a world-wide truth, "*Ach, Herr, der Ackerbauer ist nie zufrieden.*" ("Ah, Sir, the farmer is never contented.")

II

THE WATERS OF MEROM

ALL day we ride along the hills skirting the marshy plain of Huleh. Here the springs and parent streams of Jordan are gathered, behind the mountains of Naphtali and at the foot of Hermon, as in a great green basin about the level of the ocean, for the long, swift rush down the sunken trench which leads to the deep, sterile bitterness of the Dead Sea.

THE SPRINGS OF JORDAN

Was there ever a river that began so fair and ended in such waste and desolation?

Here in this broad, level, well-watered valley, along the borders of these vast beds of papyrus and rushes intersected by winding, hidden streams, Joshua and his fierce clans of fighting men met the Kings of the north with their horses and chariots, "at the waters of Merom," in the last great battle for the possession of the Promised Land. It was a furious conflict, the hordes of footmen against the squadrons of horsemen; but the shrewd command that came from Joshua decided it: "Hough their horses and burn their chariots with fire." The Canaanites and the Amorites and the Hittites and the Hivites were swept from the field, driven over the western mountains, and the Israelites held the Jordan from Jericho to Hermon. (Joshua xi:1–15.)

The springs that burst from the hills to the left of our path and run down to the sluggish channels of the marsh on our right are abundant and beautiful.

Here is 'Ain Mellâha, a crystal pool a hundred yards wide, with wild mint and watercress growing around it, white and yellow lilies floating on its surface, and great fish showing themselves in the transparent open spaces among the weeds, where the water bubbles up from the bottom through dancing hillocks of clean, white sand and shining pebbles.

Here is 'Ain el-Belâta, a copious stream breaking forth from the rocks beneath a spreading terebinth-tree, and rippling down with merry rapids toward the jungle of rustling reeds and plumed papyrus.

While luncheon is preparing in the shade of the terebinth, I wade into the brook and cast my fly along the ripples. A couple of ragged, laughing, bare-legged Bedouin boys follow close behind me, watching the new sport with wonder. The fish are here, as lively and gamesome as brook trout, plump, golden-sided fellows ten or twelve inches long. The feathered hooks tempt them, and they rise freely to the lure. My tattered pages are greatly excited, and make impromptu pouches in the breast of their robes, stuffing in the fish until they look quite fat. The catch is enough for a good supper for their whole family, and a dozen more for a delicious fish-salad at our camp that night. What kind of fish are they?

I do not know: doubtless something Scriptural and Oriental. But they taste good; and so far as there is any record, they are the first fish ever taken with the artificial fly in the sources of the Jordan.

The plain of Huleh is full of life. Flocks of waterfowl and solemn companies of storks circle over the swamps. The wet meadows are covered with herds of black buffaloes, wallowing in the ditches, or staring at us sullenly under their drooping horns. Little bunches of horses, and brood mares followed by their long-legged, awkward foals, gallop beside our cavalcade, whinnying and kicking up their heels in the joy of freedom. Flocks of black goats clamber up the rocky hillsides, following the goatherd who plays upon his rustic pipe quavering and fantastic music, softened by distance into a wild sweetness. Small black cattle with white faces march in long files across the pastures, or wander through the thickets of bulrushes and papyrus and giant fennel, appearing and disappearing as the screen of broad leaves and trembling plumes close behind them.

A few groups of huts made out of wattled reeds stand beside the sluggish watercourses, just as they did when Macgregor in his Rob Roy canoe attempted to explore this impenetrable morass forty years ago. Along the higher ground are lines of black Bedouin tents, arranged in transitory villages.

These flitting habitations of the nomads, who come down from the hills and lofty deserts to fatten their flocks and herds among unfailing pasturage, are all of one pattern. The low, flat roof of black goats' hair is lifted by the sticks which support it, into half a dozen little peaks, perhaps five or six feet from the ground. Between these peaks the cloth sags down, and is made fast along the edges by intricate and confusing guy-ropes. The tent is shallow, not more than six feet deep, and from twelve to thirty feet long, according to the wealth of the owner and the size of his family,—two things which usually correspond. The sides and the partitions are sometimes made of woven reeds, like coarse matting. Within there is an apartment (if you can call it so) for the family, a pen for the chickens, and room for dogs, cats, calves and other creatures to find shelter. The fireplace of flat stones is in the centre, and the smoke oozes out through the roof and sides.

The Bedouin men, in flowing *burnous* and *keffi-yeh*, with the '*agâl* of dark twisted camel's hair like a crown upon their heads, are almost all handsome: clean-cut, haughty faces, bold in youth and dignified in old age. The women look weatherbeaten and withered beside them. Even when you see a fine face in the dark blue mantle or under the white head-dress, it is almost always disfigured by purplish tattooing around the lips and chin. Some of the younger girls are beautiful, and most of the children are entrancing.

They play games in a ring, with songs and clapping hands; the boys charge up and down among the tents with wild shouts, driving a round bone or a donkey's hoof with their shinny-sticks; the girls chase one another and hide among the bushes in some primeval form of "tag" or "hide-and-seek."

A merry little mob pursues us as we ride through each encampment, with outstretched hands and half-jesting, half-plaintive cries of "*Bakhshîsh! bakhshîsh!*" They do not really expect anything. It is only a part of the game. And when the Lady holds out her open hand to them and smiles as she repeats, *"Bakhshîsh! bakhshîsh!"* they take the joke quickly, and run away, laughing, to their sports.

At one village, in the dusk, there is an open-air wedding: a row of men dancing; a ring of women and girls looking on; musicians playing the shepherd's pipe and the drum; maidens running beside us to beg a present for the invisible bride: a rude charcoal sketch of human society, primitive, irrepressible, confident, encamped for a moment on the shadowy border of the fecund and unconquerable marsh.

Thus we traverse the strange country of Bedouinia, travelling all day in the presence of the Great Sheikh of Mountains, and sleep at night on the edge of a little village whose name we shall never know. A dozen times we ask George for the real name of that place, and a dozen times he repeats it for us with painstaking courtesy; it sounds like a compromise between a cough and a sneeze.

III

WHERE JORDAN RISES

THE Jordan is assembled in the northern end of the basin of Huleh under a mysterious curtain of tall, tangled water-plants. Into that ancient and impenetrable place of hiding and blending enter many little springs and brooks, but the main sources of the river are three.

The first and the longest is the Hasbâni, a strong, foaming stream that comes down with a roar from the western slope of Hermon. We cross it by the double arch of a dilapidated Saracen bridge, looking down upon thickets of oleander, willow, tamarisk and woodbine.

The second and largest source springs from the rounded hill of Tel el-Kâdi, the supposed site of the ancient city of Dan, the northern border of Israel. Here the wandering, landless Danites, finding a country to their taste, put the too fortunate inhabitants of Leshem to the sword and took possession. And here King Jereboam set up one of his idols of the golden calf.

There is no vestige of the city, no trace of the idolatrous shrine, on the huge mound which rises thirty or forty feet above the plain. But it is thickly covered with trees: poplars and oaks and wild figs and acacias and wild olives. A pair of enormous veterans, a valonia oak and a terebinth, make a broad bower of shade above the tomb of an unknown Mohammedan saint, and there we eat our midday meal, with the murmur of running waters all around us, a clear rivulet singing at our feet, and the chant of innumerable birds filling the vault of foliage above our heads.

After lunch, instead of sleeping, two of us wander into the dense grove that spreads over the mound. Tiny streams of water trickle through it: blackberry-vines and wild grapes are twisted in the undergrowth; ferns and flowery nettles and mint grow waist-high. The main spring is at the western base of the mound. The water comes bubbling and whirling out from under a screen of wild figs and vines, forming a pool of palest, clearest blue, a hundred feet in diameter. Out of this pool the new-born river rushes, foaming and shouting down the hillside, through lines of flowering styrax and hawthorn and willows trembling over its wild joy.

The third and most impressive of the sources of Jordan is at Bâniyâs, on one of the foothills of Hermon. Our path thither leads us up from Dan, through high green meadows, shaded by oak-trees, sprinkled with innumerable blossoming shrubs and bushes, and looking down upon the lower fields blue with lupins and vetches, or golden with yellow chrysanthemums beneath which the red glow of the clover is dimly burning like a secret fire.

Presently we come, by way of a broad, natural terrace where the white encampment of the Moslem dead lies gleaming beneath the shade of mighty oaks and terebinths, and past the friendly olive-grove where our own tents are standing, to a deep ravine filled to the brim with luxuriant verdure of trees and vines and ferns. Into this green cleft a little river, dancing and singing, suddenly plunges and disappears, and from beneath the veil of moist and trembling leaves we hear the sound of its wild joy, a fracas of leaping, laughing waters.

An old Roman bridge spans the stream on the

The Approach to Baniyas.

brink of its downward leap. Crossing over, we ride
through the ruined gateway of the town of Bâniyâs,
turn to right and left among its dirty, narrow
streets, pass into a leafy lane, and come out in
front of a cliff of ruddy limestone, with niches and
shrines carved on its face, and a huge, dark cavern
gaping in the centre.

A tumbled mass of broken rocks lies below the
mouth of the cave. From this slope of débris, sixty
or seventy feet long, a line of springs gush forth in
singing foam. Under the shadow of trembling poplars and broad-boughed sycamores, amid the lush
greenery of wild figs and grapes, bracken and briony and morning-glory, drooping maidenhair and
flower-laden styrax, the hundred rills swiftly run
together and flow away with one impulse, a full-
grown little river.

There is an immemorial charm about the place
Mysteries of grove and fountain, of cave and hilltop,
bewitch it with the magic of Nature's life, ever
springing and passing, flowering and fading, basking
in the open sunlight and hiding in the secret places
of the earth. It is such a place as Claude Lorraine

might have imagined and painted as the scene of one of his mythical visions of Arcadia; such a place as antique fancy might have chosen and decked with altars for the worship of unseen dryads and nymphs, oreads and naiads. And so, indeed, it was chosen, and so it was decked.

Here, in all probability, was Baal-Gad, where the Canaanites paid their reverence to the waters that spring from underground. Here, certainly, was Paneas of the Greeks, where the rites of Pan and all the nymphs were celebrated. Here Herod the Great built a marble temple to Augustus the Tolerant, on this terrace of rock above the cave. Here, no doubt, the statue of the Emperor looked down upon a strange confusion of revelries and wild offerings in honour of the unknown powers of Nature.

All these things have withered, crumbled, vanished. There are no more statues, altars, priests, revels and sacrifices at Bâniyâs—only the fragment of an inscription around one of the votive niches carved on the cliff, which records the fact that the niche was made by a certain person who at that time was "Priest of Pan." *But the name of this person who wished to be remembered is precisely the part of the carving which is illegible.*

Ironical inscription! Still the fountains gush from the rocks, the poplars tremble in the breeze, the sweet incense rises from the orange-flowered styrax, the birds chant the joy of living, the sunlight and the moonlight fall upon the sparkling waters, and the liquid starlight drips through the glistening leaves.

But the Priest of Pan is forgotten, and all that old interpretation and adoration of Nature, sensuous, passionate, full of mingled cruelty and ecstasy, has melted like a mist from her face, and left her serene and pure and lovely as ever.

Here at Paneas, after the city had been rebuilt by Philip the Tetrarch and renamed after him and his Imperial master, there came one day a Peasant of Galilee who taught His disciples to draw near to Nature, not with fierce revelry and superstitious awe, but with tranquil confidence and calm joy. The goatfoot god, the god of panic, the great god Pan, reigns no more beside the upper springs of Jordan. The name that we remember here, the name that makes the message of flowing stream and sheltering tree and singing bird more clear and cool and sweet to our hearts, is the name of Jesus of Nazareth.

IV

CÆSAREA PHILIPPI

Yes, this little Mohammedan town of Bâniyâs, with its twoscore wretched houses built of stones from the ancient ruins and huddled within the broken walls of the citadel, is the ancient site of Cæsarea Philippi. In the happy days that we spend here, rejoicing in the most beautiful of all our camps in the Holy Land, and yielding ourselves to the full charm of the out-of-doors more perfectly expressed than we had ever thought to find it in Palestine,—in this little paradise of friendly trees and fragrant flowers,

> "at snowy Hermon's foot,
> Amid the music of his waterfalls,"—

the thought of Jesus is like the presence of a comrade, while the memories of human grandeur and transience, of man's long toil, unceasing conflict, vain pride and futile despair, visit us only as flickering ghosts.

We climb to the top of the peaked hill, a thousand feet above the town, and explore the great Crusaders' Castle of Subeibeh, a ruin vaster in extent and nobler in situation than the famous *Schloss* of Heidelberg. It not only crowns but completely covers the summit of the steep ridge with the huge drafted stones of its foundations. The immense round towers, the double-vaulted gateways, are still standing. Long flights of steps lead down to subterranean reservoirs of water. Spacious courtyards, where the knights and men-at-arms once exercised, are transformed into vegetable gardens, and the passageways between the north citadel and the south citadel are travelled by flocks of lop-eared goats.

From room to room we clamber by slopes of crumbling stone, discovering now a guard-chamber with loopholes for the archers, and now an arched chapel with the plaster intact and faint touches of colour still showing upon it. Perched on the high battlements we look across the valley of Huleh and the springs of Jordan to Kal'at Hûnîn on the mountains of Naphtali, and to Kal'at esh-Shakîf above the gorge of the River Litâni.

From these three great fortresses, in the time of the Crusaders, flashed and answered the signal-fires of the chivalry of Europe fighting for possession of Palestine. What noble companies of knights and ladies inhabited these castles, what rich festivals were celebrated within these walls, what desperate struggles defended them, until at last the swarthy hordes of Saracens stormed the gates and poured over the defences and planted the standard of the crescent on the towers and lit the signal-fires of Islam from citadel to citadel.

All the fires have gone out now. The yellow whin blazes upon the hillsides. The wild fig-tree splits the masonry. The scorpion lodges in the deserted chambers. On the fallen stone of the Crusaders' gate, where the Moslem victor has carved his Arabic inscription, a green-gray lizard poises motionless, like a bronze figure on a paper-weight.

We pass through the southern entrance of the village of Bâniyâs, a massive square portal, rebuilt

Bridge Over the River Litani.

by some Arab ruler, and go out on the old Roman bridge which spans the ravine. The aqueduct carried by the bridge is still full of flowing water, and the drops which fall from it in a fine mist make a little rainbow as the afternoon sun shines through the archway draped with maidenhair fern. On the stone pavement of the bridge we trace the ruts worn two thousand years ago by the chariots of the men who conquered the world. The chariots have all rolled by. On the broken edge of the tower above the gateway sits a ragged Bedouin boy, making shrill, plaintive music with his pipe of reeds.

We repose in front of our tents among the olive-trees at the close of the day. The cool sound of running streams and rustling poplars is on the moving air, and the orange-golden sunset enchants the orchard with mystical light. All the swift visions of striving Saracens and Crusaders, of conquering Greeks and Romans, fade away from us, and we see the figure of the Man of Nazareth with His little company of friends and disciples coming up from Galilee.

It was here that Jesus retreated with His few faithful followers from the opposition of the Scribes and Pharisees. This was the northernmost spot of earth ever trodden by His feet, the longest distance from Jerusalem that He ever travelled. Here in this exquisite garden of Nature, in a region of the Gentiles, within sight of the shrines devoted to those Greek and Roman rites which were so luxurious and so tolerant, four of the most beautiful and significant events of His life and ministry took place.

He asked His disciples plainly to tell their secret thought of Him—whom they believed their Master to be. And when Peter answered simply: "Thou art the Christ, the Son of the living God," Jesus blessed him for the answer, and declared that He would build His church upon that rock.

Then He took Peter and James and John with Him and climbed one of the high and lonely slopes of Hermon. There He was transfigured before them, His face shining like the sun and His garments glistening like the snow on the mountain-peaks. But when they begged to stay there with Him, He led them down to the valley again, among the sinning and suffering children of men.

At the foot of the mount of transfiguration He healed the demoniac boy whom his father had brought to the other disciples, but for whom they had been unable to do anything; and He taught them that the power to help men comes from faith and prayer.

And then, at last, He turned His steps from this safe and lovely refuge, (where He might surely have lived in peace, or from which He might have gone out unmolested into the wide Gentile world), backward to His own country, His own people, the great, turbulent, hard-hearted Jewish city, and the fate which was not to be evaded by One who loved sinners and came to save them. He went down into Galilee, down through Samaria and Perea, down to Jerusalem, down to Gethsemane and to Golgotha,—fearless, calm,—sustained and nourished by that secret food which satisfied His heart in doing the will of God.

It was in the quest of this Jesus, in the hope of somehow drawing nearer to Him, that we made our pilgrimage to the Holy Land. And now, in the cool of the evening at Cæsarea Philippi, we ask ourselves whether our desire has been granted, our hope fulfilled?

Yes, more richly, more wonderfully than we dared to dream. For we have found a new vision of Christ, simpler, clearer, more satisfying, in the freedom and reality of God's out-of-doors.

Not through the mists and shadows of an infinite regret, the sadness of sweet, faded dreams and hopes that must be resigned, as Pierre Loti saw the phantom of a Christ whose irrevocable disappearance has left the world darker than ever!

Not amid strange portents and mysterious rites, crowned with I know not what aureole of traditionary splendours, founder of elaborate ceremonies and centre of lamplit shrines, as Matilde Serao saw the image of that Christ whom the legends of men have honoured and obscured!

The Jesus whom we have found is the Child of Nazareth playing among the flowers; the Man of Galilee walking beside the lake, healing the sick, comforting the sorrowful, cheering the lonely and despondent; the well-beloved Son of God transfigured in the sunset glow of snowy Hermon, weeping by the sepulchre in Bethany, agonizing in the moonlit garden of Gethsemane, giving His life for those who did not understand Him, though they loved Him, and for those who did not love Him because they did not understand Him, and rising at last triumphant over death,—such a Saviour as all men need and as no man could ever have imagined if He had not been real.

His message has not died away, nor will it ever die. For confidence and calm joy He tells us to turn to Nature. For love and sacrifice He bids us live close to our fellowmen. For comfort and immortal hope He asks us to believe in Him and in our Father, God.

That is all.

But the bringing of that heavenly message made the country to which it came the Holy Land. And the believing of that message, to-day, will lead any child of man into the kingdom of heaven. And the keeping of that faith, the following of that Life, will transfigure any country beneath the blue sky into a holy land.

THE PSALM OF A SOJOURNER

Thou hast taken me into the tent of the world, O God:
Beneath thy blue canopy I have found shelter:
Therefore thou wilt not deny me the right of a guest.

Naked and poor I arrived at the door before sunset:
Thou hast refreshed me with beautiful bowls of milk:
As a great chief thou hast set forth food in abundance.

I have loved the daily delights of thy dwelling:
Thy moon and thy stars have lighted me to my bed:
In the morning I have found joy with thy servants.

Surely thou wilt not send me away in the darkness?
There the enemy Death is lying in wait for my soul:
Thou art the host of my life and I claim thy pro-
*   tection.*

Then the Lord of the tent of the world made answer:
The right of a guest endureth but for an appointed
*   time:*
After three days and three nights cometh the day of
*   departure.*

288

*Yet hearken to me since thou fearest the foe in the
    dark:*
*I will make with thee a new covenant of everlasting
    hospitality:*
*Behold I will come unto thee as a stranger and be thy
    guest.*

*Poor and needy will I come that thou mayest entertain
    me:*
*Meek and lowly will I come that thou mayest find a
    friend:*
*With mercy and with truth will I come to give thee
    comfort.*

*Therefore open the door of thy heart and bid me wel-
    come:*
*In this tent of the world I will be thy brother of the
    bread:*
*And when thou farest forth I will be thy companion
    forever.*

Then my soul rested in the word of the Lord:
*And I saw that the curtains of the world were
    shaken,*
*But I looked beyond them to the eternal camp-fires
    of my friend.*

XII

THE ROAD TO DAMASCUS

I

THROUGH THE LAND OF THE DRUSES

YOU may go to Damascus now by rail, if you like, and have a choice between two rival routes, one under government ownership, the other built and managed by a corporation. But to us encamped among the silvery olives at Bâniyâs, beside the springs of Jordan, it seemed a happy circumstance that both railways were so far away that it would have taken longer to reach them than to ride our horses straight into the city. We were delivered from the modern folly of trying to save time by travelling in a conveyance more speedy than picturesque, and left free to pursue our journey in a leisurely, independent fashion and by the road that would give us most pleasure. So we chose the longer way, the northern path around Mount Hermon, through the country of the Druses, instead of the more frequented road to the east by Kafr Hawar.

How delightful is the morning of such a journey!

The fresh face of the world bathed in sparkling dew; the greetings from tent to tent as we four friends make our rendezvous from the far countries of sleep; the relish of breakfast in the open air; the stir of the camp in preparation for a flitting; canvas sinking to the ground, bales and boxes heaped together, mule-bells tinkling through the grove, horses refreshed by their long rest whinnying and nipping at each other in play—all these are charming variations and accompaniments to the old tune of "Boots and Saddles."

The immediate effect of such a setting out for a day's ride is to renew in the heart those "vital feelings of delight" which make one simply and inexplicably glad to be alive. We are delivered from those morbid questionings and exorbitant demands by which we are so often possessed and plagued as by some strange inward malady. We feel a sense of health and harmony diffused through body and mind as we ride over the beautiful terrace which slopes down from Bâniyâs to Tel-el Kâdi.

We are glad of the green valonia oaks that spread

their shade over us, and of the blossoming hawthorns that scatter their flower-snow on the hillside. We are glad of the crested larks that rise
warbling from the grass, and of the buntings and
chaffinches that make their small merry music in
every thicket, and of the black and white chats that
shift their burden of song from stone to stone
beside the path, and of the cuckoo that tells his name
to us from far away, and of the splendid bee-eaters
that glitter over us like a flock of winged emeralds
as we climb the rocky hill toward the north. We
are glad of the broom in golden flower, and of the
pink and white rock-roses, and of the spicy fragrance
of mint and pennyroyal that our horses trample out
as they splash through the spring holes and little
brooks. We are glad of the long, wide views westward over the treeless mountains of Naphtali and
the southern ridges of the Lebanon, and of the
glimpses of the ruined castles of the Crusaders, Kal'at
esh-Shakîf and Hûnîn, perched like dilapidated
eagles on their distant crags. Everything seems to
us like a personal gift. We have the feeling of ownership for this day of all the world's beauty. We

could not explain or justify it to any sad philosopher who might reproach us for unreasoning felicity. We should be defenceless before his arguments and indifferent to his scorn. We should simply ride on into the morning, reflecting in our hearts something of the brightness of the birds' plumage, the cheerfulness of the brooks' song, the undimmed hyaline of the sky, and so, perhaps, fulfilling the Divine Intention of Nature as well as if we chose to becloud our mirror with melancholy thoughts.

We are following up the valley of the longest and highest, but not the largest, of the sources of the Jordan: the little River Hâsbânî, a strong and lovely stream, which rises somewhere in the northern end of the Wâdi et-Teim, and flows along the western base of Mount Hermon, receiving the tribute of torrents which burst out in foaming springs far up the ravines, and are fed underground by the melting of the perpetual snow of the great mountain. Now and then we have to cross one of these torrents, by a rude stone bridge or by wading. All along the way Hermon looks down upon us from his throne, nine thousand feet in air. His head is wrapped in a turban of spotless white, like a Druse chieftain, and his snowy winter cloak still hangs down over his shoulders, though its lower edges are already fringed and its seams opened by the warm suns of April.

Presently we cross a bridge to the west bank of the Hâsbânî, and ride up the delightful vale where poplars and mulberries, olives, almonds, vines and figs, grow abundantly along the course of the river. There are low weirs across the stream for purposes of irrigation, and a larger dam supplies a mill with power. To the left is the sharp barren ridge of the Jebel ez-Zohr separating us from the gorge of the River Lîtânî. Groups of labourers are at work on the watercourses among the groves and gardens. Vine-dressers are busy in the vineyards. Plough-men are driving their shallow furrows through the stony fields on the hillside. The little river, here in its friendliest mood, winds merrily among the plantations and orchards which it nourishes, making a cheerful noise over beds of pebbles, and humming a deeper note where the clear green water plunges over a weir.

We have now been in the saddle five hours; the sun is ardent; the temperature is above eighty-five degrees in the shade, and along the bridle-path there is no shade. We are hungry, thirsty, and tired. As we cross the river again, splashing through a ford, our horses drink eagerly and attempt to lie down in the cool water. We have to use strong persuasion not only with them, but also with our own spirits, to pass by the green grass and the sheltering olive-trees on the east bank and push on up the narrow, rocky defile in which Hâsbeiyâ is hidden. The bridle-path is partly paved with rough cobblestones, hard and slippery, which make the going weariful. The heat presses on us like a burden. Things that would have delighted us in the morning now give us no pleasure. We have made the greedy traveller's mistake of measuring our march by the extent of our endurance instead of by the limit of our enjoyment.

Hâsbeiyâ proves to be a rather thriving and picturesque town built around the steep sides of a bay or opening in the valley. The amphitheatre of hills is terraced with olive-orchards and vineyards. There are also many mulberry-trees cultivated for the silkworms, and the ever-present figs and almonds are not wanting. The stone houses of the town rise, on winding paths, one above the other, many of them having arched porticoes, red-tiled roofs, and green-latticed windows. It is a place of about five thousand population, now more than half Christian, but formerly one of the strongholds and capitals of the mysterious Druse religion.

Our tents are pitched at the western end of the town, on a low terrace where olive-trees are growing. When we arrive we find the camp surrounded and filled with curious, laughing children. The boys are a little troublesome at first, but a word from an old man who seems to be in charge brings them to order, and at least fifty of them, big and little, squat in a semicircle on the grass below the terrace, watching us with their lustrous brown eyes.

They look full of fun, those young Druses and Maronites and Greeks and Mohammedans, so I try a mild joke on them, by pretending that they are a class and that I am teaching them a lesson. "A, B, C," I chant, and wait for them to repeat after me. They promptly take the lesson out of my hands and recite the entire English alphabet in chorus, winding up with shouts of "Goot mornin'! How you do?" and merry laughter. They are all pupils from the mission schools which have been established since the great Massacre of 1860, and which are helping, I hope, to make another forever impossible.

One of our objects in coming to Hâsbeiyâ was to ascend Mount Hermon. We send for the Druse guide and the Christian guide; both of them assure us that the adventure is impossible on account of the deep snow, which has increased during the last fortnight. We can not get within a mile of the summit. The snow will be waist-deep in the hollows. The mountain is inaccessible until June. So, after exchanging visits with the missionaries and seeing something of their good work, we ride on our way the next morning.

II

RÂSHEIYÂ AND ITS AMERICANISM

THE journey to Râsheiyâ is like that of the preceding day, except that the bridle-paths are rougher and more precipitous, and the views wider and more splendid. We have crossed the Hâsbânî again, and leaving the Druses' valley, the Wâdi et-Teim, behind us, have climbed the high table-land to the west. We did not know why George Cavalcanty led us away from the path marked in our Baedeker, but we took it for granted that he had some good reason. It is well not to ask a wise dragoman all the questions that you can think of. Tell him where you want to go, and let him show you how to get there. Certainly we are not inclined to complain of the longer and steeper route by which he has brought us, when we sit down at lunch-time among the limestone crags and pinnacles of the wild upland and look abroad upon a landscape which offers the grandeur of immense outlines and vast distances, the beauty of a crystal clearness in all its infinitely

varied forms, and the enchantment of gemlike colours, delicate, translucent, vivid, shifting and playing
in hues of rose and violet and azure and purple and
golden brown and bright green, as if the bosom of
Mother Earth were the breast of a dove, breathing
softly in the sunlight.

As we climb toward Râsheiyâ we find ourselves going back a month or more into early spring.
Here are the flowers that we saw in the Plain of
Sharon on the first of April, gorgeous red anemones, fragrant purple and white cyclamens, delicate
blue irises. The fig-tree is putting forth her tender
leaf. The vines, lying flat on the ground, are bare
and dormant. The springing grain, a few inches
long, is in its first flush of almost dazzling green.

The town, built in terraces on three sides of a
rocky hill, 4,100 feet above the sea, commands an
extensive view. Hermon is in full sight; snow-
capped Lebanon and Anti-Lebanon face each
other for forty miles; and the little lake of Kafr Kûk
makes a spot of blue light in the foreground.

We are camped on the threshing-floor, a level meadow beyond and below the town; and there the Râs-

heiyan gilded youth come riding their blooded horses in the afternoon, running races over the smooth turf and showing off their horsemanship for our benefit.

There is something very attractive about these Arabian horses as you see them in their own country. They are spirited, fearless, sure-footed, and yet, as a rule, so docile that they may be ridden with a halter. They are good for a long journey, or a swift run, or a *fantasia*. The prevailing colour among them is gray, but you see many bays and sorrels and a few splendid blacks. An Arabian stallion satisfies the romantic ideal of how a horse ought to look. His arched neck, small head, large eyes wide apart, short body, round flanks, delicate pasterns, and little feet; the way he tosses his mane and cocks his flowing tail when he is on parade; the swiftness and spring of his gallop, the dainty grace of his walk— when you see these things you recognise at once the real, original horse which the painters used to depict in their "Portraits of General X on his Favourite Charger."

I asked Calvalcanty what one of these fine creatures would cost. "A good horse, two or three hundred dollars; an extra-good one, four hundred; a fancy one, who knows?"

We find Râsheiyâ full of Americanism. We walk out to take photographs, and at almost every street corner some young man who has been in the United States or Canada salutes us with: "How are you to-day? You fellows come from America? What's the news there? Is Bryan elected yet? I voted for McKinley. I got a store in Kankakee. I got one in Jackson, Miss." A beautiful dark-eyed girl, in a dreadful department-store dress, smiles at us from an open door and says: "Take my picture? I been at America."

One talkative and friendly fellow joins us in our walk; in fact he takes possession of us, guiding us up the crooked alleys and out on the housetops which command the best views, and showing us off to his friends,—an old gentleman who is spinning goats' hair for the coarse black tents (St. Paul's trade), and two ladies who are grinding corn in a hand-mill, one pushing and the other pulling. Our self-elected guide has spent seven years in Illinois and Indiana, peddling and store-keeping. He has returned to Râsheiyâ as a successful adventurer and built a stone house with a red roof and an arched portico. Is he going to settle down there for life? "I not know," says he. "Guess I want sell my house now. This country beautiful; I like look at her. But America free—good government—good place to live. Gee whiz! I go back quick, you bet."

III

ANTI-LEBANON AND THE RIVER ABANA

Our path the next day leads up to the east over the ridges of the slight depression which lies between Mount Hermon and the rest of the Anti-Lebanon range. We pass the disconsolate village and lake of Kafr Kûk. The water which shone so blue in the distance now confesses itself a turbid, stagnant pool, locked in among the hills, and breeding fevers for those who live beside it. The landscape grows wild and sullen as we ascend; the hills are strewn with shattered fragments of rock, or worn into battered and fantastic crags; the bottoms of the ravines

305

are soaked and barren as if the winter floods had
just left them. Presently we are riding among
great snowdrifts. It is the first day of May. We
walk on the snow, and pack a basketful on one of
the mules, and pelt each other with snowballs.

We have gone back another month in the calendar
and are now at the place where "winter lingers in
the lap of spring." Snowdrops, crocuses, and little
purple grape-hyacinths are blooming at the edge
of the drifts. The thorny shrubs and bushes, and
spiny herbs like astragalus and cousinia, are green-
stemmed but leafless, and the birds that flutter
among them are still in the first rapture of vernal
bliss, the gay music that follows mating and pre-
cedes nesting. Big dove-coloured partridges, beautifully marked with black and red, are running
among the rocks. We are at the turn of the year,
the surprising season when the tide of light and life
and love swiftly begins to rise.

From this Alpine region we descend through
two months in half a day. It is mid-March on a
beautiful green plain where herds of horses were
feeding around an encampment of black Bedouin

tents; the beginning of April at Khân Meithelûn, on the post-road, where there are springs, and poplar-groves, in one of which we eat our lunch, with lemonade cooled by the snows of Hermon; the end of April at Dimas, where we find our tents pitched upon the threshing-floor, a levelled terrace of clay looking down upon the flat roofs of the village.

Our camp is 3,600 feet above sea-level, and our morning path follows the telegraph-poles steeply down to the post-road, and so by a more gradual descent along the hard and dusty turnpike toward Damascus. The landscape, at first, is bare and arid: rounded reddish mountains, gray hillsides, yellowish plains faintly tinged with a thin green. But at El-Hâmi the road drops into the valley of the Baradâ, the far-famed River Abana, and we find ourselves in a verdant paradise.

Tall trees arch above the road; white balconies gleam through the foliage; the murmur and the laughter of flowing streams surround us. The railroad and the carriage-road meet and cross each other down the vale. Country houses and cafés, some dingy and dilapidated, others new and trim, are half hidden among the groves or perched close beside the high-way. Poplars and willows, plane-trees and lindens, walnuts and mulberries, apricots and almonds, twisted fig-trees and climbing roses, grow joyfully wherever the parcelled water flows in its many channels. Above this line, on the sides of the vale, everything is bare and brown and dry. But the depth of the valley is an embroidered sash of bloom laid across the sackcloth of the desert. And in the centre of this long verdure runs the parent river, a flood of clear green; rushing, leaping, curling into white foam; filling its channel of thirty or forty feet from bank to bank, and making the silver-leafed willows and poplars, that stand with their feet in the stream, tremble with the swiftness of its cool, strong current. Truly Naaman the Syrian was right in his boasting to the prophet Elisha: Abana, the river of Damascus, is better than all the waters of Israel.

The vale narrows as we descend along the stream, until suddenly we pass through a gateway of steep cliffs and emerge upon an open plain beset with mountains on three sides. The river, parting into seven branches, goes out to water a hundred and fifty square miles of groves and gardens, and we follow the road through the labyrinth of rich and luscious green. There are orchards of apricots enclosed with high mud walls; and open gates through which we catch glimpses of crimson rose-trees and scarlet pomegranates and little fields of wheat glowing with blood-red poppies; and hedges of white hawthorn and wild brier; and trees, trees, trees, everywhere embowering us and shutting us in.

Presently we see, above the leafy tops, a sharp-pointed minaret with a golden crescent above it. Then we find ourselves again beside the main current of the Baradâ, running swift and merry in a walled channel straight across an open common, where soldiers are exercising their horses, and donkeys and geese are feeding, and children are playing, and dyers are sprinkling their long strips of blue cotton cloth laid out upon the turf beside the river. The road begins to look like the commence-ment of a street; domes and minarets rise before us; there are glimpses of gray walls and towers, a few shops and open-air cafés, a couple of hotel signs. The river dives under a bridge and disappears by a hundred channels beneath the city, leaving us at the western entrance of Damascus.

IV

THE CITY THAT A LITTLE RIVER MADE

I CANNOT tell whether the river, the gardens, and the city would have seemed so magical and entrancing if we had come upon them in some other way or seen them in a different setting. You can never detach an experience from its matrix and weigh it alone. Comparisons with the environs of Naples or Florence visited in an automobile, or with the suburbs of Boston seen from a trolley-car, are futile and unilluminating.

The point about the Baradâ is that it springs full-born from the barren sides of the Anti-Lebanon, swiftly creates a paradise as it runs, and then disappears absolutely in a wide marsh on the edge of the desert.

The point about Damascus is that she flourishes

on a secluded plain, the Ghûtah, seventy miles from the sea and twenty-three hundred feet above it, with no *hinterland* and no sustaining provinces, no political leadership, and no special religious sanctity, with nothing, in fact, to account for her distinction, her splendour, her populous vitality, her self-sufficing charm, except her mysterious and enduring quality as a mere city, a hive of men. She is the oldest living city in the world; no one knows her birthday or her founder's name. She has survived the empires and kingdoms which conquered her,—Nineveh, Babylon, Samaria, Greece, Egypt—their capitals are dust, but Damascus still blooms "like a tree planted by the rivers of water." She has given her name to the reddest of roses, the sweetest of plums, the richest of metal-work, and the most lustrous of silks; her streets have bubbled and eddied with the currents of

> the multitudinous folk
> That do inhabit her and make her great.

She is the typical city, pure and simple, of the Orient, as New York or San Francisco is of the

Occident: the open port on the edge of the desert, the trading-booth at the foot of the mountains, the pavilion in the heart of the blossoming bower,—the wonderful child of a little river and an immemorial Spirit of Place.

Every time we go into the city, (whether from our tents on the terrace above an ancient and dilapidated pleasure-garden, or from our red-tiled rooms in the good Hôtel d'Orient, to which we had been driven by a plague of sand-flies in the camp), we step at once into a chapter of the "Arabian Nights' Entertainments."

It is true, there are electric lights and there is a trolley-car crawling around the city; but they no more make it Western and modern than a bead necklace would change the character of the Venus of Milo. The driver of the trolley-car looks like one of "The Three Calenders," and a gayly dressed little boy beside him blows loudly on an instrument of discord as the machine tranquilly advances through the crowd. (A man was run over a few months ago; his friends waited for the car to come around the next day, pulled the driver from his

312

perch, and stuck a number of long knives through him in a truly Oriental manner.)

The crowd itself is of the most indescribable and engaging variety and vivacity. The Turkish soldiers in dark uniform and red fez; the cheerful, grinning water-carriers with their dripping, bulbous goatskins on their backs; the white-turbaned Druses with their bold, clean-cut faces; the bronzed, impassive sons of the desert, with their flowing mantles and bright head-cloths held on by thick, dark rolls of camel's hair; the rich merchants in their silken robes of many colours; the picturesquely ragged beggars; the Moslem pilgrims washing their heads and feet, with much splashing, at the pools in the marble courtyards of the mosques; the merry children, running on errands or playing with the water that gushes from many a spout at the corner of a street or on the wall of a house; the veiled Mohammedan women slipping silently through the throng, or bending over the trinkets or fabrics in some open-fronted shop, lifting the veil for a moment to show an olive-tinted cheek and a pair of long, liquid brown eyes; the bearded Greek priests

313

in their black robes and cylinder hats; the Christian women wrapped in their long white sheets, but with their pretty faces uncovered, and a red rose or a white jasmine stuck among their smooth, shining black tresses; the seller of lemonade with his gaily decorated glass vessel on his back and his clinking brass cups in his hand, shouting, *"A remedy for the heat,"*—*"Cheer up your hearts,"*—*"Take care of your teeth";* the boy peddling bread, with an immense tray of thin, flat loaves on his head, crying continually to Allah to send him customers; the seller of turnip-pickle with a huge pink globe upon his shoulder looking like the inside of a pale watermelon; the donkeys pattering along between fat burdens of grass or charcoal; a much-bedizened horseman with embroidered saddle-cloth and glittering bridle, riding silent and haughty through the crowd as if it did not exist; a victoria dashing along the street at a trot, with whip cracking like a pack of firecrackers, and shouts of, *"O boy! Look out for your back! your foot! your side!"*—all these figures are mingled in a passing show of which we never grow weary.

The long bazaars, covered with a round, wooden archway rising from the second story of the houses, are filled with a rich brown hue like a well-coloured meerschaum pipe; and through this mellow, brumous atmosphere beams of golden sunlight slant vividly from holes in the roof. An immense number of shops, small and great, shelter themselves in these bazaars, for the most part opening, without any reserve of a front wall or a door, in frank invitation to the street. On the earthen pavement, beaten hard as cement, camels are kneeling, while the merchants let down their corded bales and display their Persian carpets or striped silks. The cook-shops show their wares and their processes, and send up an appetising smell of lamb *kibâbs* and fried fish and stuffed cucumbers and stewed beans and okra, and many other dainties preparing on diminutive charcoal grills.

In the larger and richer shops, arranged in semi-European fashion, there are splendid rugs, and embroideries old and new, and delicately chiselled brasswork, and furniture of strange patterns lavishly inlaid with mother-of-pearl; and there I go with the Lady to study the art of bargaining as practised between the trained skill of the Levant and the native genius of Walla Walla, Washington. In the smaller and poorer bazaars the high, arched roofs give place to tattered awnings, and sometimes to branches of trees; the brown air changes to an atmosphere of brilliant stripes and patches; the tiny shops, (hardly more than open booths), are packed and festooned with all kinds of goods, garments and ornaments: the chafferers conduct their negotiations from the street, (sidewalk there is none), or squat beside the proprietor on the little platform of his stall.

The custom of massing the various trades and manufactures adds to the picturesque joy of shopping or dawdling in Damascus. It is like passing through rows of different kinds of strange fruits. There is a region of dangling slippers, red and yellow, like cherries; a little farther on we come to a long trellis of clothes, limp and pendulous, like bunches of grapes; then we pass through a patch of saddles, plain and coloured, decorated with all sorts of beads and tinsel, velvet and morocco, lying

A Small Bazaar in Damascus.

on the ground or hung on wooden supports, like big, fantastic melons.

In the coppersmiths' bazaar there is an incessant clattering of little hammers upon hollow metal. The goldsmiths sit silent in their pens within a vast, dim building, or bend over their miniature furnaces making gold and silver filigree. Here are the carpenters using their bare feet in their work almost as deftly as their fingers; and yonder the dyers festooning their long strips of blue cotton from their windows and balconies. Down there, on the way to the Great Mosque, the booksellers hold together: a dwindling tribe, apparently, for of the thirty or forty shops which were formerly theirs not more than half a dozen remain true to literature: the rest are full of red and yellow slippers. Damascus is more inclined to loafing or to dancing than to reading. It seems to belong to the gay, smiling, easy-going East of Scheherazade and Aladdin, not to the sombre and reserved Orient of fierce mystics and fanatical fatalists.

Yet we feel, or imagine that we feel, the hidden presence of passions and possibilities that belong to the tragic side of life underneath this laughing mask of comedy. No longer ago than 1860, in the great Massacre, five thousand Christians perished by fire and shot and dagger in two days; the streets ran with blood; the churches were piled with corpses; hundreds of Christian women were dragged away to Moslem harems; only the brave Abd-el-Kader, with his body-guard of dauntless Algerine veterans, was able to stay the butchery by flinging himself between the blood-drunken mob and their helpless victims.

This was the last wholesale assassination of modern times that a great city has seen, and prosperous, pleasure-loving, insouciant Damascus seems to have quite forgotten it. Yet there are still enough wild Kurdish shepherds, and fierce Bedouins of the desert, and riffraff of camel-drivers and herdsmen and sturdy beggars and homeless men, among her three hundred thousand people to make dangerous material if the tiger-madness should break loose again. A gay city is not always a safe city. The Lady and I saw a man stabbed to death at noon, not fifty feet away from us, in a street beside the Ottoman Bank.

318

Nothing is safe until justice and benevolence and tolerance and mutual respect are diffused in the hearts of men. How far this inward change has gone in Damascus no one can tell. But that some advance has been made, by real reforms in the Turkish government, by the spread of intelligence and the enlightenment of self-interest, by the sense of next-doorness to Paris and Berlin and London, which telegraphs, railways, and steamships have produced, above all by the useful work of missionary hospitals and schools, and by the humanizing process which has been going on inside of all the creeds, no careful observer can doubt. I fear that men will still continue to kill each other, for various causes, privately and publicly. But thank God it is not likely to be done often, if ever again, in the name of Religion!

The medley of things seen and half understood has left patterns damascened upon my memory with intricate clearness: immense droves of camels coming up from the wilderness to be sold in the market; factories of inlaid woodwork and wrought brasswork in which hundreds of young children, with beautiful

and seeming-merry faces, are hammering and fil-
ing and cutting out the designs traced by the
draughtsmen who sit at their desks like schoolmas-
ters; vast mosques with rows of marble columns,
and floors covered with bright-coloured rugs, and
files of men, sometimes two hundred in a line, with
a leader in front of them, making their concerted
genuflections toward Mecca; costly interiors of
private houses which outwardly show bare whitewashed walls, but within welcome the stranger to
hospitality of fruits, coffee, and sweetmeats, in
stately rooms ornamented with rich tiles and precious
marbles, looking upon arcaded courtyards fragrant
with blossoming orange-trees and musical with
tinkling fountains; tombs of Moslem warriors and
saints,—Saladin, the Sultan Beibars, the Sheikh
Arslân, the philosopher Ibn-el-Arabi, great fighters
now quiet, and restless thinkers finally satisfied;
public gardens full of rose-bushes, traversed by
clear, swift streams, where groups of women sit gossiping in the shade of the trees or in little kiosques,
the Mohammedans with their light veils not altogether hiding their olive faces and languid eyes, the

Christians and Jewesses with bare heads, heavy necklaces of amber, flowers behind their ears, silken dresses of soft and varied shades; cafés by the river, where grave and important Turks pose for hours on red velvet divans, smoking the successive cigarette or the continuous nargileh. Out of these memory-pictures of Damascus I choose three.

The Lady and I are climbing up from the great Mosque of the Ommayyades into the Minaret of the Bride, at the hour of 'Asr, or afternoon prayer. As we tread the worn spiral steps in the darkness we hear, far above, the chant of the choir of muezzins, high-pitched, long-drawn, infinitely melancholy, calling the faithful to their devotions.

"*Allah akbar! Allah akbar! Allah is great! I testify there is no God but Allah, and Mohammed is the prophet of Allah! Come to prayer!*"

The plaintive notes float away over the city toward all four quarters of the sky, and quaver into silence. We come out from the gloom of the staircase into the dazzling light of the balcony which runs around the top of the minaret. For a few moments we can see little; but when the first bewilderment passes, we are conscious that all the charm and wonder of Damascus are spread at our feet.

The oval mass of the city lies like a carving of old ivory, faintly tinged with pink, on a huge table of malachite. The setting of groves and gardens, luxuriant, interminable, deeply and beautifully green, covers a circuit of sixty miles. Beyond it, in sharpest contrast, rise the bare, fawn-coloured mountains, savage, intractable, desolate; away to the west, the snow-crowned bulk of Hermon; away to the east, the low-rolling hills and slumbrous haze of the desert. Under these flat roofs and white domes and long black archways of bazaars three hundred thousand folk are swarming. And there, half emerging from the huddle of decrepit modern buildings and partly hidden by the rounded shed of a bazaar, is the ruined top of a Roman arch of triumph, battered, proud, and indomitable.

An hour later we are scrambling up a long, shaky ladder to the flat roofs of the joiners' bazaar, built close against the southern wall of the Mosque. We walk across the roofs and find the ancient south door of the Mosque, now filled up with masonry, and almost completely concealed by the shops above which we are standing. Only the entablature is visible, richly carved with garlands. Kneeling down, we read upon the lintel the Greek inscription in uncial letters, cut when the Mosque was a Christian church. The Moslems who are bowing and kneeling and stretching out their hands toward Mecca among the marble pillars below, know nothing of this inscription. Few even of the Christian visitors to Damascus have ever seen it with their own eyes, for it is difficult to find and read. But there it still endures and waits, the bravest inscription in the world: *"Thy kingdom, O Christ, is a kingdom of all ages, and Thy dominion lasts throughout all generations."*

From this eloquent and forgotten stone my memory turns to the Hospital of the Edinburgh Medical Mission. I see the lovely garden full of roses, columbines, lilies, pansies, sweet-peas, strawberries just in bloom. I see the poor people coming in a steady stream to the neat, orderly dispensary; the sweet, clean wards with their spotless beds; the merciful candour and completeness of the operating-room; the patient, cheerful, vigorous, healing ways of the great Scotch doctor, who limps around on his broken leg to minister to the needs of other folk. I see the little group of nurses and physicians gathered on Sunday evening in the doctor's parlour for an hour of serious, friendly talk, hopeful and happy. And there, amid the murmur of Abana's rills, and close to the confused and glittering mystery of the Orient, I hear the music of a simple hymn:

> "Dear Lord and Father of mankind,
>   Forgive our foolish ways!
>   Reclothe us in our rightful mind,
>   In purer lives thy service find,
>   In deeper reverence, praise.
>
> "O Sabbath rest by Galilee!
>   O calm of hills above,
>   Where Jesus knelt to share with Thee
>   The silence of eternity
>   Interpreted by love!

324

THE ROAD TO DAMASCUS

"Drop thy still dews of quietness,
    Till all our strivings cease;
Take from our souls the strain and stress,
And let our ordered lives confess
    The beauty of Thy peace."